FATAL PRINCESS

RETRIBUTION GAMES BOOK 4

ELLA MILES

RETRIBUTION GAMES SERIES

Mistaken Hero
Forbidden Princess
Tempted Hero
Fatal Princess
Tortured Hero
Dangerous Princess

1

RI

Odette's alive.

I barely remember or understand what part I played in it all, even after Odette told me the truth.

I didn't kill Odette despite what everyone in this room thought. I didn't harm her. I helped her, although Beckett might see that as just as much of a betrayal.

It's not a betrayal I deserve to die for, and yet he was going to kill me for killing his wife. He didn't give me a chance to explain myself. He didn't even try to figure out why I would have done such a thing.

Nothing.

He just dragged me here in front of everyone and was about to shoot me dead tied to a pole, even after I saved his life.

It didn't matter.

It didn't matter that I loved him or that I thought he loved me.

None of it mattered—for Beckett, it was always *her*. He loved her more than anything, even when he found out she was lying to him. I wasn't allowed such luxuries.

Because of *her*.

Odette is currently gripping his hand like she never left. Like she's loved him the entire time she's been lying to him.

Beckett doesn't bat her hand away. He holds hers right back. He still loves her. He'd die for her.

She just left him.

She's not worthy of his love, but I'm not going to be the one to explain that to him. If he's too big of an idiot to see how she's playing him, then that's on him. They deserve each other.

The only problem is my heart—my stupid fucking heart. It fell in love with a man who loved another woman. A man who would never love me no matter what. A man who used me to find her. A man who would have killed me to get what he wanted.

I stare at their joined hands—thump, thump, thump—and my heart still beats for him. Still yearns for him. Still has a sliver of hope that I'm missing something. He couldn't have possibly planned on killing me, right?

My brain reminds me—I'm still tied to this pole, and she has him.

I don't know what happens next. One minute I'm tied to the post, stupidly yearning for a man I can never have—the wrong man—and the next, chaos erupts all around us.

I can't understand what the crowd is shouting or why they're all rushing the stage.

I don't look at Beckett. I can't look at him, but I do look at the rest of the guys. Hayes, Lennox, and Gage all have their weapons drawn. Caius's jaw is on the floor as he stares at his sister—alive.

A bullet flies past my cheek.

Fuck.

I have no time to sit here and wallow in self-pity. I have to get free of these chains, or I'm going to end up dead.

I tug on the metal clasps, but they're solid. I'm not strong enough to break them.

I push my hands up the pole until I can reach my head. Digging around in my nest of hair, I desperately search for a bobby pin—the most useful of hair accessories. I almost always have a pin stuck in my hair for these very situations. Luckily, I find one quickly.

I push the bobby pin into the lock, twisting it around until I feel the chains drop away. I'm free, although I don't have much chance of getting out of here alive.

I don't have any weapons. Even though Odette is alive, I don't trust that no one here still wants to kill me. With the fighting all around me, a rift in the organization has clearly exploded with lots of battling opinions and goals.

My only hope is to slip out of here undetected.

I'm about to jump off the stage when I hear Gage say, "This way, Princess."

Is he talking to me?

I flip my head over my shoulder as I crouch on the edge of the stage, about to run in the opposite direction. I don't trust Gage. I don't trust any of them. They brought me here. They tied me to the pole. They were going to watch while Beckett killed me.

Gage frowns when he sees my expression. Hayes looks heartbroken. Even Lennox looks disgusted with himself as he watches me.

"I don't trust you—any of you!" I scream at them.

Gage tosses me a gun, and I catch it in midair. I cock my head and stare at him.

He doesn't say anything. He doesn't beg me to trust him. He offers me a choice completely my own—jump off the stage and fight my own way out or take the help he and the others are offering.

Another bullet flies by. I don't have time to think through my decision, so I go with my gut and follow Gage.

Gage holds out his hand to help me off the stage, but I don't take it. I jump down behind him, landing hard on my feet.

Hayes and Lennox follow after, each with their gun out and flanking me like they will shoot anyone who comes close to us.

I'm not sure I believe them. This is their family, after all. Most of the people here belong to the Retribution Kings. The guys grew up with these people, vowed to protect them. They wouldn't shoot their family to protect me.

Gage pushes through the crowd, and I follow tightly after, hoping no one will notice us making our escape. I'm also praying I wasn't a fool, and Gage isn't just leading me somewhere for Beckett to finish me off after the fighting is over.

A man's eyes widen instantly as we pass.

He notices me.

I hold my breath. I don't have a great angle to shoot him, but I lift my gun anyway, hoping to kill him before he shoots me.

A shot from behind me beats us both, and I watch the man fall to the ground. I turn my head in time to see Lennox lowering his gun. Lennox shot him—a Retribution King—to save me.

I gape at Lennox, stumbling to a stop.

"Keep moving, Princess," Lennox says with a smirk. His eyes twinkle with amusement, enjoying proving me wrong.

"This doesn't mean I trust you—any of you," I say.

"We know, but that's just because we kept you in the dark of our real plan," Hayes says.

Real plan?

I glare as I search Hayes's eyes for an answer. "What do you mean?"

"Enough," Gage says sternly. "We have to keep moving. We aren't safe yet."

He's right.

There will be a time for questions later.

Now we have to get somewhere safe.

Our pulses race as we move through the crowd as quietly and discreetly as possible. Thankfully, there is enough fighting and gunfire that no one else seems to notice us as we weave through the mass of people.

Hayes suddenly hisses from behind us.

I stop, turning toward him to find a red gash appear on his cheek.

"Keep moving! Don't stop," Hayes says.

We move faster, trying to avoid any more stray bullets as we run through the auditorium.

"This way!" Gage shouts back at us.

He ducks into a corridor, and we all follow. The sound of gunfire immediately softens as we enter a tunnel.

There's a door at the end of the tunnel that leads outside, but Gage doesn't lead us that way. Instead, he runs his hand along the wall as we walk. He stops suddenly, popping a door in the wall open.

"Where does that lead?" I ask, stopping suddenly.

"To your safety," Gage answers vaguely.

I frown at him as I stare down the dark tunnel. *Do I go down this hidden tunnel or out the main exit?*

I hear the crowd getting louder, and I know they are headed this way. I need to decide.

I take a step toward the tunnel, but none of the guys move to follow. "Are you guys not coming with me?"

Gage shakes his head. "You'll pop out in an abandoned house. There's a car there that can take you anywhere you want, but we have to stay here. We can't be seen with you." He rubs the back of his head. "Not right now, at least."

I nod slowly, understanding.

"Thank you for getting me this far."

"It was the least we could do," Lennox says.

I look to Hayes, his cheek now covered in blood. "Get that looked at."

He smiles brightly. "Of course, Princess. Now get the hell out of here. We'll see you soon enough."

I smile back and am about to step into the tunnel when a voice rings down the hallway.

"Fighter, wait!"

Beckett is running down the corridor toward us. I don't see Odette, but I assume she's right behind him. His eyes are big with concern, and he's clearly out of breath. There's blood on his shirt, but I don't care.

At least, that's what I tell myself—I. Don't. Care. About. Beckett.

He keeps running down the corridor. "Wait!"

My heart skips a beat.

I want to wait.

I want to hear him out.

I want to know what the hell happened back there.

I want to give him the benefit of the doubt.

But I can't.

I just can't.

I can't go there with him again.

He fucked up.

I'm done.

I'm in this for myself from now on.

I look to Gage, trying to figure out if he's going to let me pass when his boss is running toward us, yelling for me to wait.

He gives the slightest of nods, and I know he won't let Beckett come after me. I don't know why, though. I don't understand any of their loyalties, not anymore, but I don't hesitate.

I run through the secret door and into the hidden tunnel. I hear the door snap behind me as I run, descending into darkness.

With each step, I wait to hear sounds of the door opening, of footsteps following, of Beckett catching up to me.

The sounds never come.

I'm free, at least for the moment. I should take the opportunity to run, to escape this world and completely disappear. But I don't want to spend my life running.

I'll stay and fight. But for now, I need one night away from all of this, and I know exactly where I'm going.

2

RI

I TREK through the tunnel for close to an hour before finally reaching the end, where a ladder leads upward. The tunnel has been completely empty except for me, so I've had plenty of time with my thoughts—not necessarily a good thing.

I've alternated between going back to find out what Beckett was going to say and going back to kill him.

Somehow, I manage to do neither of those things and keep walking. I climb up the ladder and press against the door above me. Carefully, I raise the wooden board and push the end of my gun out before popping my head out.

I scan the small bedroom surrounding me. I've come up just beside a bed, so I can't see much. Slowly and silently, I hoist myself up and look around the edge of the bed. The room's empty.

I stand and move to the door of the bedroom. I press my ear against it and listen once again.

Nothing.

I need to keep moving. I can't stay in this house. *Who*

knows how many of the Retribution Kings know about this escape hatch and will come looking for me here?

I move silently through the house, finding a set of keys hanging by the back door. I grab the keys and head into the garage, where I find an old car.

It will do.

I climb in and start driving, knowing exactly where I'm going. I'm not going to run, not really, but I need a break. I need one night to relax. Tomorrow, I go to war again.

I drive quickly, assuming the car is traceable, but it doesn't matter. Soon everyone will know where I've gone. It will just be a matter of which of my enemies decides to come for me first.

When I arrive at my apartment, I'm exhausted. So much has happened since I was last here, but all I want is to see Lucy. I need to see my friend, the one little part of my life that's normal. I need to warn her to get away. She's not safe being my friend, not anymore.

I knock on the door, so I don't scare Lucy by barging in. It takes her a minute to come to the door, but as soon as she sees that it's me, I'm tackled inside the room by both her and Loki.

I laugh, knowing I made the right decision to come here. I'm sure Vincent, the Retribution Kings, and every other gang is monitoring my apartment, but I don't care.

"What are you doing here? And you look—"

"Like a mess?"

She nods.

I sigh. "It's a long story, but I thought I'd spend as much time as I have with you." I don't mention her leaving, not yet. Vincent has used her to control me my entire life. Every man in the competition could use her to control me.

I need her somewhere safe or at least safer. She'll resist. She always does. But I'm hoping this time she might listen to me.

"Go shower, get cleaned up. I'll get the ice cream ready, and then you can tell me all about it."

I nod without smiling. "Don't answer the door if anyone comes. Just come get me."

"I won't answer the door," she says slowly, realizing I'm not out of danger.

When I'm satisfied she won't open the door, and no one is coming in the next five minutes, I head to my bathroom to shower.

I take far too short of a shower, but I don't want to leave Lucy alone and unprotected. And I want to maximize what little time I have left with her.

I throw on some comfy sweats and an oversized T-shirt before throwing my hair up in a messy bun. Then I head back to the living room, where I find Loki snuggled up next to Lucy on the couch. She holds up a pint of chocolate chip cookie dough ice cream to me.

I take the pint and spoon from her with a smile.

She takes a bite of her own Cherry Garcia ice cream. "So, want to tell me what happened?"

I shake my head. "The usual crap. But it's different this time, Luce. I think you should consider leaving. Go to Australia, or Switzerland, or Thailand, anywhere you want. Just somewhere far away where it will be harder to get you."

Lucy frowns. "I'm not going anywhere, and neither are you."

"Why not?"

She moves the ice cream around in her pint but doesn't answer right away. "Because I'm not in danger."

"You are."

"I'm not. Trust me, Vincent won't let anything happen to me."

I frown. "He's threatened you my entire life."

She shakes her head. "There is so much you don't know, Ri. So much."

"What are you talking about? What aren't you telling me?"

She bites her lip and tucks her long blonde hair behind her ear as she considers her next words. "I'm sorry, but I can't tell you—my safety depends on it. But I'm not in danger. And you can't run. You have to stay. You have to find the best guy to marry."

"I'm not going to marry any of them. They all suck."

Lucy's quiet, too quiet.

"Luce, talk to me. You're scaring me."

She shakes her head and shoves more ice cream into her mouth, staring blankly at the wall across from us.

I set my own ice cream container down on the end table, and then I grab her shoulders, forcing her to look at me. "What do you know?"

She swallows hard, and her bottom lip trembles. I tuck her hair behind her ear, trying to comfort her.

"Who threatened you?"

"No one. I'm fine. Just listen to me—stay in the game, marry the best man, and after it's all over, you can find a way to get out."

My eyes cut back and forth over hers as I read between the lines of her words, searching for what she's not telling me. The only way Lucy stays alive is if I finish the game. If I don't, Vincent will kill her.

I pull her into a hug.

"I will. I'm not running."

Lucy hugs me tighter. "I'm not running either."

"Fine. Let's eat our ice cream and watch an action movie to take our minds off things."

Lucy scrunches her face in disgust.

I laugh, falling back onto the couch. "Horror movie?"

"No way."

I frown. "Comedy?"

"Romantic comedy."

I sigh. The last thing I want is any movie that reminds me of Beckett or love, but I settle into the couch as Lucy picks out a sappy movie.

I eat my ice cream slowly, savoring every bite and barely paying attention to the movie on the screen. Being back in this apartment reminds me of other things, of the last time I was here with Beckett, of fucking him for the first time.

I don't regret it, I realize. I don't regret any of it—any of the kisses, the touches, the fucking, none of it.

I should regret it—my heart now feels like it's been stabbed by a million tiny little knives that will never heal —but I don't. For a moment, he made me feel alive. He made me believe there were good men out there and that it was worth fighting to be the one to choose the man I spend the rest of my life with.

The sounds of footsteps in the hallway rush to my ears, despite the blare of the television. Someone's here.

Beckett?

The other guys?

Vincent?

Someone else from the game?

Who?

The footsteps fade, though—someone who lives in the apartment building. No one is coming for me.

That's a lie. Everyone is coming for me. It's just a matter of who comes first and when.

Every footstep, every sound, every door slam from the hallway has me on edge. Lucy obliviously watches the movie, unaware of any of the danger.

Whoever comes, they won't come for her. I'll make sure of it. She'll be safe. That's the only thing I can get right, keeping her safe. She's been my friend for so long that I'll do anything for her.

There's a knock on the door.

A knock.

"Lucy, take Loki and go to your bedroom."

She doesn't ask questions, calmly doing as I said.

I walk toward the door with my gun, ready to shoot whoever is behind the door. If it's Beckett, I'll shoot him in the groin, and then he can explain to me why he almost killed me for a crime I didn't commit.

I chuckle inwardly at that thought.

My guess is it's Beckett or Gage and the rest of the guys. No one else would knock. The assholes in my life would barge in and try to take me as their captive.

I open the door, expecting Beckett.

Instead, I find Ryker leaning against my doorframe with a soft smile on his face.

3

BECKETT

THE LOOK on Ri's face as I run to her will haunt me for all of my days. Her gaunt face, tear-streaked eyes, and stern frown broke my heart. I can see how I'd broken hers. Not just broken, but I shattered her heart beyond repair. The damage I did—I won't be able to fix it, not as long as I live.

The thought shatters what's left of my own heart as I watch her disappear into the tunnel.

It's clear what Ri thought—I was going to kill her. She didn't see the truth. For that, I can never be forgiven.

Gage snaps the door shut behind her as I reach the guys.

"Where is she going?" I ask.

The guys all look to Gage. He's the one who appears to be making the decisions at the moment.

"Somewhere safe," he answers.

I take a deep breath. I want to know where. I want to go to her immediately, but we have bigger problems at the moment.

"Promise she'll be safe," I ask, my voice cracking, my

body screaming to run after her as I stare at the space in the wall where she disappeared.

"Ri will be safe. No one knows about this tunnel except us, Caius, and his father. This was an emergency escape for the leader. She'll be safe," Gage says.

I nod.

"Who was attacking?" Lennox asks.

"The Retribution Kings. They were mad with what I did."

"Our own people were attacking? Are you sure?" Hayes asks.

I nod.

"Jesus Christ. We need to get out of here then," Hayes says.

I agree.

"Beckett!" her voice sends chills down my spine. It's a voice I've longed to hear again. I've wanted to hear her voice for so fucking long, but now it sounds like nails on a chalkboard.

I turn in time to see Odette and Caius running toward us. They're out of breath when they finally reach us.

"How the hell are you alive?" Lennox asks, staring at Odette with anger in his eyes.

I look around the group, and it seems everyone except for Caius has a stern glare on their face as they stare at Odette.

"We need to get somewhere safe first, then Odette can explain what happened. We can go back to my place," Caius says, placing a comforting hand on her back.

"No," I say.

All eyes are on me.

"We go to the cabin. It's further away and safer. Your condo will be the first place they look," I say.

Caius opens his mouth to argue, but he sees the look on my face and doesn't say anything.

We all start jogging out toward our cars when I feel a hand brush against mine. I glance down to see Odette's fingers threading through mine.

My hand goes cold at the sight, and I harshly pull my hand away.

She frowns at me.

I don't want to think about the truth—we are still legally married. And yet she's tricked me and lied to me—god knows what the truth is.

We make it to the SUV, and all pile in. Lennox takes the driver's seat, and I take the front passenger seat. I don't want to sit for an hour next to Odette while we drive.

Gage and Hayes climb in the back, and Caius sits next to Odette in the middle row, comforting her like she just survived extreme torture. Although from the looks of her, she looks pretty damn healthy to me. Not a mark, scar, or bruise is visible on her skin.

I turn on the radio as soon as Lennox starts driving, making it clear to everyone there will be no talking until we get to the cabin. I should be thinking about the repercussions of my actions. About the men that will be coming after us or about how Odette is alive, but all I can think about is Ri. I hope like hell she's run far, far away from here.

Because if I have to watch her forced to marry another man when the games are over, I'm not sure I can handle it. I'm not sure I can handle watching her go through any more pain.

Lennox pulls up to the cabin far too soon.

"It's safe," Gage says from the backseat.

We all climb out and head inside, going straight for

the liquor. I pour myself a drink, not bothering to ask anyone else if they want one before walking out onto the back deck.

I need plenty of fresh air and a lot of fucking alcohol in my system before I have this conversation.

Odette is the first to find me outside.

She walks toward me with her arms outstretched, expecting me to welcome her home. She expects me to hug her, to love her again. But the truth is I'm not sure if I ever loved her in the first place.

Instead of holding her, I lift my drink to my mouth as I stare at her. She gets the hint and stops.

"I—" she starts.

"Wait until everyone else is out here. That way, you only have to tell your story once."

She frowns. "You don't want privacy?"

"No."

I pace on the deck while she quietly takes a seat on one of the wicker chairs. Everyone else files out quickly and sits on the various chairs and benches. I'm the only one who remains standing, leaning against a post.

"Start talking, Odette, and don't leave anything out," I snap, more fury spewing out of my lips than I realized I had.

She looks to Caius and then back to me, taking a deep breath. "Before our wedding, there was a death threat against me, a plot to kill me. My father's condition was poor, and we knew he wouldn't survive much longer, so we couldn't postpone the wedding."

"Who is we?" I ask, interrupting.

Her eyes flutter to Caius. "My father, Caius, and me."

I frown. Caius knew more than he was telling me—the bastard.

I take a long sip of my whiskey.

Odette fidgets with the ends of the strands of her hair, but she continues. "We knew you and I needed to get married and initiate you in as the leader as soon as possible. But we also had to protect me, so we also changed the date of the wedding—to throw everyone off. And as soon as the wedding was over, I needed to disappear."

"Disappear maybe, but die?" I growl.

"Disappearing wouldn't have helped. They would have still come after me. I had to die in order to stay alive. And you had to think I was dead—everyone did—in order for our plan to work. If you weren't devastated, no one would have believed I was dead."

I have so many questions, but I start with, "Who are they? Who wanted you dead and why?"

"Vincent Corsi. He's been trying to destroy the Retribution Kings for years. We cause the most conflict with the various gangs when we take retribution into our own hands. My father almost started an all-out war between the gangs, and Corsi wasn't happy about it. He wanted to teach my father a lesson in retribution to show that he had all the power in this city. He wants the Retribution Kings under his control, so he called for my death."

"You knew Odette was alive?" I ask Caius.

"No, I didn't. I knew that her life was at risk and that she was going to try and disappear, but after I saw those horrible photos, I thought she was dead—same as you," Caius says.

I don't know if I believe him, but I want to hear more of what Odette has to say.

"How did you fake your death? And how did Ri come into this?" I ask.

Odette sighs.

"I hated leaving on our wedding night, but I knew that's when it had to be done. I needed blood—a lot of blood. So I drew my own blood and spread it around the room to make it look like I'd been dangerously close to death when I was taken. But I needed an attacker, someone Caius and my father wouldn't recognize. I couldn't just use anyone."

"How did you rope Ri into this?" I ask, losing patience with her.

"After she interrupted our wedding, I knew she was exactly who I was looking for. I didn't realize she was a Corsi; that was just a bonus. I just thought she was a scared girl in need of some money. Once I told her my story, she agreed to help me without payment."

She takes a deep breath and then continues. "I knew you'd go downstairs to get my medicine, so that's when I had Rialta come to my room. She pretended to fight me, to threaten me. She did cut my skin and make me bleed, but I was willing to endure that in order to survive."

"So then you spent your time on some private island living the good life while everyone here thought you were dead? The fake photos of your bloody body were a nice touch. Whose body did we bury? Did you kill someone to pretend they were you?" I rage.

I'm pissed, beyond pissed. I can't believe she would do this to me. I can't believe I ever loved this woman. I can't fucking believe I fell in love with a monster.

"The body was a woman who died of cancer, similar age and build."

I shake my head as I pace. "Where have you been all this time?"

"My plan was to run, to always be running. I'd wait

tables, bartend, clean houses, pick up any job I could to survive. I thought I'd be giving you a better life. You could take over as leader—I knew you'd be amazing at it, Beckett. You deserved to be the leader, needed to be the leader of the Retribution Kings.

"But I also knew that you deserved to find someone who didn't lie to you, someone you chose to love, not a fake like me. I did love you, and I still do, but I didn't think I was enough. So I thought the best plan was to fake my death—save myself and let you live your life." Her voice is practically shaking now.

Caius goes to her and puts his arms around her shoulders, tucking her into his side. He stares at me like he can't believe I'm not the one holding her right now.

Everyone else stays in their seats, though, watching her closely. I can't read any of their faces. I don't know if they trust her or not, but I know what I believe.

"Stop your tears. You chose to leave. You chose to keep me in the dark when I could have easily protected you and kept you safe. You ran. You chose to go it alone. You didn't give me a chance to decide if I really loved you despite the lies."

Odette pushes Caius off her shoulders as she stomps toward me with fire in her eyes. I don't cower. I don't back down, even though I'm pretty sure she's about to slap me.

"You have no idea what I've been through these past few weeks!" she yells.

"And you have no idea the pain I've been through!"

She frowns and pulls up her sleeves, revealing a plethora of scars and bruises on her arms. "I was free a grand total of one week before I was taken. I was tortured and raped and abused. My life was threatened every night, and I wasn't sure if I was going to wake up the next morning or die in my sleep. I've spent every day regretting my decision. Every day realizing the mistake I made in not trusting you. It's made me realize how much I love you. I'd do anything for you."

I narrow my eyes as I study her bruises—they're real enough, but that doesn't mean I believe her story.

"How did you escape?" I ask. She grew up in this world. She could have had as much training and skill as Ri, but I doubt that.

"I was released with a warning to you. You have to step down as leader of the Retribution Kings. Otherwise, they will kidnap me again and actually kill me."

Her story is a mess, full of reasons not to believe her. Not to mention she has never told me the truth in her life, so I don't trust a word she says without undeniable proof. Even then, I'm not sure I'll believe her, not when I saw a video of Ri killing her, and it turned out to be a lie.

But I have one question left. There's only one question that could give me some answers.

"Who took you?"

Her nostrils flare as she thinks of the evil who took her. "Enzo Black."

4

RI

"WHAT ARE YOU DOING HERE?" I ask Ryker as we both stand in the doorway of my apartment.

Looking at his black, mid-length hair and devilish grin, he's the last person I expected here. Ryker has a reputation as one of the cruelest leaders, but after he offered up two of his men to help me, I'm not sure if his reputation is warranted. It doesn't mean I trust him either, though.

"I won the game."

Oh, shit. He's here to collect his prize—me.

"You can go to hell. I'm not going to let you kidnap me, treat me as your possession, and then let you rape me. I'll kill you first. Ask Leighton what happened to his men when he tried it." I slam the door in his face, but he catches it with his hand.

I aim my gun at him, expecting him to do the same, followed by a dozen men filing into my apartment. Instead, Ryker puts his hands up in the air.

"I'm not here to kidnap you. And I would never think of raping or hurting a woman."

I frown. "Your reputation says differently."

"And your reputation is that of a damsel in distress, nothing more than a princess who can't take care of herself. Neither of our reputations tells the whole truth."

I don't drop my aim as he slowly enters our apartment, his hands still up.

"I'm here to protect you," he says.

"Why?"

"You're my responsibility for the week. If anything happens to you, Corsi will have my head, and my men will be without a leader once again. So my loyalty is to you for the week. I will do everything in my power to keep you safe."

He seems genuine, but I don't trust him. I don't trust anyone—not after Beckett betrayed me, the only man I thought I could love.

He puts his hands down, but I don't drop my gun.

"I'll take you and Lucy wherever you want, but you can't stay in this apartment. It's not safe. Too many people know about it, and too many people will come looking for you."

"How do you know about Lucy?"

"I did my due diligence."

I was right. Everyone knows about Lucy, and she's not safe.

"You'll take us anywhere?"

"Anywhere." He nods.

"Even if I wanted to go to a rival gang? You'd take me there? Make sure we were safe?"

"I promise to take you wherever you want to go. You will not be a prisoner with me. If you want to go back to Beckett, I'll take you."

I don't ask how he knows that's where I would want to go.

"If you betray us if you fail to keep us safe, if you trap us or hurt either of us in any way, I will kill you. My father and I will ruin your entire gang and everyone you love, do you understand?"

Ryker smiles. "Of course, why else do you think I'm here? The goodness of my heart? I may like you, but I wouldn't be risking my life to protect you if it didn't serve my own self-interest."

His smile is what gets me. It's so genuine and sweet, not to mention the light behind his eyes. He plays the villain well. I've seen his monster act firsthand, but his men respected him and wanted to work for him.

This could be an epic mistake, but then again, I'm used to making epic mistakes. I wish I could rely entirely on myself, but I don't have a choice. There are too many people that want me and will have no problem hurting Lucy to control me.

I'll go with him for now, but that doesn't mean I'll trust him.

"Take us to a private house rental. Pay in cash. Only you are allowed to know the location, no one else." It's a lot to ask. He'd be lying to his men, hiding the truth from them. I don't expect him to agree.

"Your wish is my command, Princess."

I frown, lowering the gun for the first time. "Don't call me Princess."

He chuckles low and deep. "Okay, Rialta."

I wince. "Don't call me Rialta either."

He raises his eyebrows. "What would you like me to call you?"

"Ri, just Ri."

"Well, Ri, give me five minutes to figure out a house we can go to and something to tell my men as to why they won't be seeing much of me this week." He pulls out his phone.

I'm still not sure I should trust him, but I accept that he won't try to shoot or kidnap me in the next five minutes, so I leave him in the living room and head to Lucy's room.

She opens the door with a frown. "No."

"No, what?"

"No, I'm not going. I have school, a job, a life. I'm not going to live in some random house with a guy I don't know. This place is impenetrable. No one will hurt me here!" She crosses her arms and sticks out her hips with a deep pout on her face.

"Luce, please," I say softly.

"No."

"Luce, how many times have I been kidnapped over the years?"

"That's not fair. I haven't—"

"Lucy," I plead with my eyes. Loki trudges over to Lucy's side and licks her hand encouragingly.

"Fine, but you're going to explain to Frank why I don't show up for work. I don't have any tests this week, so it shouldn't be that big of a deal if I miss class. And I get the best room."

I smile. "Done."

She rolls her eyes and then stomps back into her room to start packing. I start to head to my room to pack as well but stop in my doorway.

"Only one bag!"

"You're no fun!" Lucy yells back, making me laugh.

I gather a backpack worth of clothes and toiletries

quickly, not really caring which clothes I pack before moving on to the more important things—weapons. I pack several knives and guns before heading back out to see if Ryker has found a place.

He looks up from his phone when he sees me. "You pack light. I like that."

The next moment, Lucy rolls out an oversized cheetah-print suitcase with Loki's dog bed and a bag of his supplies sitting on top.

Ryker frowns, rubbing the back of his head as he stares at her. "We're going to be gone less than a week. Is all that shit really necessary?"

"Yes," Lucy spits back.

Well, there isn't going to be any love lost between the two of them.

Loki decides to take a moment to inspect the new person in our apartment. I expect him to bark or jump on him. Instead, he wags his tail as he licks Ryker's hand.

"Huh," Lucy says, looking at Loki's reaction and then to me.

Maybe I was right to trust Ryker, but it's still too soon to let my guard down. I won't let the fact that Loki seems to like him mean I give him my full trust. Loki also liked Beckett, and he almost killed me.

"Found a place?" I ask Ryker.

"I did." He holds out his phone to me.

I take it and see a house listing that says sold. I scrunch my nose. "You bought a house? How did you make this happen so quickly?"

"I'm always looking for new safe houses. I bought this one last week. No one knows about it but me. It's fully furnished and safe. But if you'd prefer me to find another place, just say the word."

His eyes are sincere. I still don't understand why he's helping me, not really. Why would he even enter the game if he doesn't have some ulterior motive?

I hand him back his phone. "This will work."

He nods, tucking his phone back in his pocket. He looks down at Lucy's bag. "You able to carry that thing? I need to be focused on our safety, not worried about your bag."

Lucy crosses her arms over her chest and huffs. "I can roll my bag just fine."

"Good. Ready, Ri?"

I nod, reaching for my gun at the same time Ryker grabs his own.

"Shoot to kill, Ri."

"I will."

"Let's go." Ryker leads the way out of my apartment, followed by Lucy rolling her bag with Loki right beside her, and I take up the rear, hoping Lucy won't get caught in any crossfire.

I don't know what awaits us. Vincent or Beckett or others might be waiting to attack us, so our only shot is to get out of here as fast as possible.

The hallway is clear, as is the garage when we make it down the elevator. We make it all the way to Ryker's car without being attacked.

Lucy and Loki climb in the back seat while Ryker and I quickly hop in front. Ryker and I are both still gripping our guns as he pulls out of the space.

"That was strange," I say.

"How was that strange? You two overreact," Lucy says from the backseat.

"No, it was strange. There are too many people after you. We should have been attacked," Ryker says.

There's an unease that circles through the car. Even Loki stills as we all stare out various windows, just waiting to be ambushed. None of the following uneventful miles we drive ease our anxieties.

And then it happens.

The car is bumped from behind. We surge forward, Ryker barely hangs onto control.

I move to point my gun out the window, but Ryker grabs my arm. "Don't put yourself in danger."

"Someone has to try and stop them."

"Then that someone is going to be me. Take the wheel."

He slides up in his seat, motioning for me to take his place. For a second, I look at him like's fucking crazy. But then the car rams into us from behind again, and I realize now isn't the time to argue his judgment.

I hop across the center console and into the seat, taking the wheel just as he pops open the driver's door and hangs from the car like a badass, and shoots at the car behind us.

I look in the rearview mirror and see the car spinning to a stop as Ryker swings back in. He rolls over my lap until he reaches the passenger's seat.

"Do you see anyone else?" I ask, gripping the wheel hard, ready for almost everything.

"There's no one behind you—"

A popping sound interrupts him, and I feel the car jerk as I drive.

"Someone hit the tires," I say, feeling the tug of the car, knowing it's not going to be drivable much longer.

Ryker turns to Lucy. "When Ri stops the car, run in the opposite direction of us. They will be focused on Ri. Run and take cover the second you can. We'll find you as soon as it's safe."

Lucy looks to me, and I nod, agreeing.

I turn the car toward an alleyway before it becomes completely undrivable. The second I stop, Lucy and Loki jump out and start running down the alley.

I reach for my door, but Ryker stops me. "Let me take the lead."

"I don't take orders, and I don't let others put their lives before mine," I say with a frown and open my door before Ryker can stop me.

Immediately, bullets fly around us as I duck behind the door and fire back.

"Do you know who they are?" I ask Ryker, who has climbed down next to me and is shooting at them.

He narrows his eyes. "They are the Lolitos."

He hesitates a moment as he looks at the men shooting at us.

I stop firing and look at him.

"You know them?"

"Some of them used to be my friends."

I frown. "Then why are they..."

"They think I'll turn on you, that I'll help them. They aren't participating in the game. They just want you dead, and Corsi's legacy destroyed."

"So why aren't you giving me to them?"

"Because I keep my promises."

He jumps out in front of our car door with a new vengeance before I can stop him. One after one, I see him take down our attackers without hesitation.

I'm frozen.

These men were his friends, and yet he's killing them all.

My mouth is agape as I watch him murder friend after friend until there is only one man left.

Ryker stares him down, aiming the gun at him, but doesn't fire.

The man facing him doesn't lower his gun, though. Instead, I see his eyes cut to me. He's about to shoot me. Despite all of his friends being killed, he doesn't think Ryker will shoot him.

Ryker's hand trembles. Whoever this person is, he means more to him than all the rest.

"Drop your gun, Hector." Ryker's voice is strong and determined, meant to show Hector how serious he is.

"She has to die, Ryker. You know that. She can't live. Corsi can't continue on. You joined the game to have their power, but we decided to destroy it, so there is no power to be gained."

"You can't shoot her. Drop. Your. Gun."

"You won't shoot me. And you definitely won't kill me. We grew up together."

"Please," Ryker says, his arm shaking so much I'm afraid even if he fires his gun, he'll miss.

I should shoot this man. I shouldn't make Ryker decide. But somehow, I can't do it. I can't be the one to end this man's life—Ryker's friend.

Maybe he'll shoot me and put me out of my misery. I've only had a broken heart for a few hours, but I can already tell it's something I can't endure for a lifetime.

I close my eyes, willing him to shoot me, to end it all right here.

I hear the pop of the gun.

I don't feel any sharp shock of pain, but then again, I'm so numb at this point I doubt a bullet would make an impact. Nothing can be as painful as a broken heart caused by broken love.

I open my eyes, looking for the wound on my body to see how long it will take for me to bleed out and die. But as I open my eyes, I can't find an obvious wound anywhere.

My heart sinks as I look out and find Ryker standing over his friend's limp body. Ryker's breathing is slow and steady, while his eyes are locked on his friend.

Ryker shot his childhood friend to protect me.

I don't understand why.

I don't understand if he's really afraid for his own life if I die or if he thinks keeping me alive is the best for his own gang. *Or maybe there's some other reason he's not telling me?*

All I know is he's going to be as broken as me now. He'll never forget this single kill as long as he lives.

Slowly, I walk over to him and place my hand gently on his shoulder.

He jumps at my touch.

I open my mouth to apologize, but I slam it shut. Nothing I say can take his pain away.

"Let's find Lucy and get out of here," Ryker says, shaking my touch off as he walks away.

I stare down at the man who wanted to kill me, the man Ryker killed to protect me. So many men have died trying to kill me, so many more will, and all for a chance to steal everything my father has worked for.

I don't know how to stop it—the unending bleeding— but I'm going to find a way. The pain and suffering have to stop, and I'm the only one who can.

5

———

BECKETT

WHEN ODETTE SAYS that Enzo Black, my half-brother and full brother in every way that matters, was the one who took her, my blood boils. It takes everything inside me not to strangle her to death right now.

She's a fucking liar.

I know she's lying. My brother would never do that. And if he did, he would tell me. It would serve some purpose. He wouldn't hurt me like this. He wouldn't make me think she was dead for weeks. Even if he was trying to help her, he would have told me the truth by now.

Or Kai would. Or Siren, Zeke, Langston, Liesel. Someone would have told me.

No, she's a liar.

I don't believe one word of her story. Not. One. Fucking. Word.

I don't know what to do next, but I do know I'm not thinking clearly. I want to kill her for what she's done, for putting Ri's life in danger.

The problem is I don't think killing Odette will solve much. It will mean I'm no longer married to her, but also

33

every Retribution King will be after me. And I can't help Ri if I'm being chased.

"Say something," Odette pleads, reaching her hand out to touch my chest.

I take a big step back rather than letting our bodies touch. If I did, she'd be dead.

"You don't want to hear what I have to say," I growl so deeply the entire forest shakes.

"Beckett, you're my husband. Of course, I want to hear what you say. I've done everything I could to get back to you. I—"

"Enough," I command.

She closes her mouth.

Caius stands behind her like he wants to kill me. I still suspect he knew more than he's letting on. I trust him about as much as I do his sister right now. I don't trust any of the Retribution Kings either.

I look around at the other guys. I do trust Gage, Lennox, and Hayes. They helped get Ri out when I couldn't. They protected her when I couldn't. And they are looking at Odette, a woman they've known all their lives, with disdain in their eyes. For now, I'll trust them.

"The Kings are here," Gage says, pulling out his phone and reviewing the perimeter of the property.

Fuck.

I knew they'd come; I just wanted enough time to hear Odette's story. I've heard it, and it's bullshit. I don't need to hear more.

"Gage, take Odette to one of the rooms and keep her there until I say otherwise."

"Baby, tell me you believe me. Tell me you still love me because I still love you," Odette tries again.

I don't say anything. Gage grabs her arm and guides

her inside the cabin. She doesn't put up much of a fight—big, fat tears stream down her cheeks and wobbly bottom lip.

It won't work on me, though. I'm heartless where she's concerned.

No, you gave your heart to another woman, a worthy woman. It's true, even if she now hates me because she thinks I betrayed her. That's really why Odette will never have my heart again.

"Lennox and Hayes, strip Caius of his weapons and lock him up in another room."

Caius moves to grab his weapons, to fight back, but they grab him before he has a chance. They've been friends a long time, so I wasn't sure if they would follow my orders or his.

Hayes grabs Caius's gun, Lennox Caius's knife. Quickly, they have his hands behind his back.

"I didn't know anything! And I believe every word of Odette's story. She was kidnapped, raped, and abused by people you call family," he yells and thrashes.

"I know, and it's why I don't trust you. I don't blame you for believing your sister," I reply.

"She's your wife!" Caius spits out as Lennox and Hayes start walking him to the door.

A roll of rage washes through me when he says 'wife.' Technically, it might be true, but she doesn't have my heart. I thought I loved her, and I was wrong. There is only one woman I love—one woman I've ever loved. And I fucked it all up by thinking I loved Odette instead.

Lennox and Hayes drag Caius away.

I follow after, heading to the front of the house to meet my fate. I check my weapons, ensuring I know where they are, but the sounds of cars and men tell me that it doesn't matter how many guns I have on me, I won't be able to fight my way out.

I walk out the front porch as I see more than a dozen men getting out of their cars.

Stan steps forward. He's one of the elders, the one who helps when I'm not around.

If they'd let me leave, I'd give him my position in a heartbeat, but I have a feeling they won't accept that. I know too much.

"Stan," I say in the way of a greeting.

"Beckett." He nods back at me. "We have a lot to discuss."

I raise an eyebrow at the men behind him. "It seems like you came here to kill me, not to talk."

"No, of course not. We came here to clear up the misunderstandings."

"Of course," I say sarcastically.

"Are you going to invite us in?"

I look out at the number of men that keep driving up. I think they're up to over twenty.

"I don't think we'll fit, and I'd rather not get blood on the upholstery. It will be a bitch to clean."

Stan laughs. "Oh, Beckett. We won't be getting any blood anywhere. We just want to talk."

"Then we can talk out here."

He sighs but doesn't fight me on it.

"What happened?"

"I don't have to defend myself. I'm the leader of the Retribution Kings. You all have to listen to me."

"That's not entirely true. We picked you as our leader, but only if you finished the final task of getting retribution. You didn't kill Rialta Corsi."

"And good thing, too, since she didn't actually kill

Odette and isn't responsible for her death. Good thing I didn't start a war because you told me to. I would have doomed us all."

Stan frowns. "So you knew Odette was alive?"

"No, I didn't, but I did my own homework. I wasn't going to kill someone without hard evidence."

"Well, we'll ignore your indiscretion because it ended up being the right thing."

"Oh, you'll ignore it, will you?" I grit out, my voice full of anger. "You wanted me as your leader; this is what you get. You have to trust that I make the right decisions for everyone."

"We do, of course, we do."

"Then why are you here?"

"To see Odette. We are overjoyed that our princess is still alive."

"She's resting. You can see her later. As you can imagine, she's had a long day."

"Sure, sure."

"Why are you here?" I growl.

"We need to finish your initiation."

"I think killing Rialta is moot now, don't you?"

"You have to complete your retribution task. We all did. We can't trust you fully until you complete it."

"What task? And if I complete it, that's it? You'll trust me fully, and there will be no more meetings like this?"

"You will have everyone in the Retribution Kings' full loyalty."

"Odette is alive. There is no need to get retribution for her. What do you want me to do?"

Stan smiles deviously.

Chills race over my arm and all over my body. I don't trust his smile.

He pulls out his phone and hands it to me.

It's a video. I'm reluctant to press play, sure of what the "evidence" is he's about to show me, but I need to see it.

I press play.

There's a grainy video of one of Enzo's yachts with Odette standing on the top deck. Enzo and Kai are on the deck too. Odette is yelling, but there is no sound. I have no idea what she's saying or where they are.

I'm sure Stan is going to make it out like Odette was kidnapped and being held against her will. This was either photoshopped, or she climbed aboard the ship just to get this footage.

I hand the phone back to him. "It's going to take more evidence than this to convince me that my brother took my wife and held her captive all this time. The last time I was shown a video like this, it wasn't the whole story. I'm not going to go after my own family until I have much more evidence."

Stan frowns.

"Enzo Black isn't your family anymore. You took a vow when you became our leader. You became a Monroe. Your loyalty should be to us, not them."

"I can be loyal to the Retribution Kings and still not kill my own brother with barely any evidence."

"Half brother—Enzo is your half brother you didn't even know about most of your life."

I want to punch the foul smirk off his face, but I don't think it would help the situation.

"I want more evidence," I grit out, trying to keep my temper at bay.

"Has Odette told you what happened?" he asks like he wasn't listening the entire time and knows exactly what Odette said to me.

I take my time answering, studying him closely. I don't know how he could have been listening, but I decide to go with the truth. "Yes, Odette told me her story."

"And what did she say?"

"That Enzo kidnapped her."

"Your own wife told you what happened. That's all the evidence you need. She told you the truth, and now you must get retribution for her."

I close my eyes, keeping my rage in, instead of letting it explode out of me. My brows pinch together, and I swear I'm getting a full-on migraine from this conversation.

"Odette just went through a very traumatic experience. I'm not sure her memories are to be relied on. We don't know if Enzo kidnapped her to hurt her or save her."

He shakes his head in disgust. "I understand that your feelings are a bit complicated, which is why we have taken it upon ourselves to study the evidence. Odette was kidnapped by Enzo Black. Your final initiation task is simple—kill Enzo Black, put an end to his empire, and then you'll be king of the Retribution Kings."

His words show how little they know. The way to end the Black Empire is not to kill Enzo; his wife, Kai, is far more in charge of things than he is.

"And if I don't?"

"You have one month to complete your new task, same as before. And if you don't, we'll kill you."

My jaw ticks, and everything clicks into place.

This is why they picked me. They've wanted Enzo dead this whole time. They wanted someone from his inner circle to have the knowledge and motivation to kill him. They didn't count on me falling out of love with Odette, though.

"Where are your men?" he asks.

"Inside resting."

"I'd like to chat with them and add some new soldiers to your ranks to help you complete your initiation task."

He tries to brush past me, but I step into his path. "I'm happy with my current team, thank you."

"You don't have a choice. Right now, I'm your second. And as a fully initiated member, I have more power than you do, especially now that you are on thin ice."

I stare at him and then out at his men. I have two choices.

One—go along with everything he says. Let him keep some of his men here as spies and basically jailers. Then I'll figure out how to get rid of them later.

Two—fight now.

The first option might be smarter, but the second option gives me a faster chance to go after Ri.

I have no idea where she is or if she's safe. What I do know is that she's pissed. She cared about me, possibly even loved me, but after what I did, she'll hate me forever. She'll never forgive me. Every second I let her keep thinking that I have less and less chance of her forgiving me, of her loving me ever again.

I look at Stan and make my choice; the only route I'm willing to take—I fight.

6

RI

WE HOTWIRED a car and found Lucy and Loki about a block away before we drove the rest of the way to Ryker's new safe house in complete silence. Not even Loki made a sound, sensing Ryker's agony and not wanting to add to it.

I drove following the in-car directions with Ryker in the passenger seat, his eyes open. Clearly, though, his mind was still on the last man—a man who was obviously a close friend. He shot and killed that friend to protect me.

I stop the car in front of a large Tudor-style mansion. None of us immediately get out as we stare up at the old home, full of character and vast rooms. There look to be so many rooms I'm afraid none of us are going to feel safe in the house.

"It has the top-of-the-line security system installed. I just finished installing it myself last week. I'll make sure it's hooked up to both of your phones too. It's a fortress, and no one knows we are here. You won't be found."

I think of the tracker I swallowed so Beckett could always find me. I consider telling Ryker but decide against it. The only man who can find me here is Beckett.

Whether I admit it or not, I want Beckett to find me, if only so I can rip out his heart for what he did to mine.

Ryker gets out, followed by Lucy and Loki, and then me.

We all get our bags. Lucy drags her large roller behind her, while Ryker and I each carry small backpacks into the large mansion.

When we enter, the vastness of the house is overwhelming. The ceiling stretches three stories up. The stairs curve up to a long sideways hallway leading each wing of the rectangular-shaped house. On the first floor, I can see rooms as far as I look in all directions.

Lucy releases Loki, who runs full speed down the first-floor hallway. She looks at Ryker. "I hope you aren't attached to any of the furniture. Loki loves to chew up new furniture."

Ryker just smiles at her. "The furniture came with the house. It was one reason I bought it. I'll sell it as soon as we leave. So no, I don't really give a damn if a couple of pieces have a few holes, dog stains, or loose threads."

Lucy laughs. "Some? More like all." She follows Loki to explore the house, leaving Ryker and me standing in the entryway.

"This house had to cost you a small fortune. Why get something so big and expensive?"

"We have a couple of small safe houses, but many of my men know where they are. This house was meant to be a safe house for as many of my men as possible. I feel it's my job to protect them, and a house like this could have done that."

"I'm sorry you wasted it on us then."

He turns to me. His body is weary, like he's just weathered a terrible storm, but he pulls strength into his eyes as he looks at me. "Don't be sorry—about anything."

And then he walks away.

I shouldn't push him, so I don't follow him. I give him space to deal with his emotions.

Lucy is loudly making food in the kitchen, and I consider spending time with her, but I'm far too exhausted for her company.

Instead, I head upstairs and choose one of the first bedrooms with an attached bathroom. I sit in the tub for a solid hour before climbing into the oversized bed, hoping sleep washes away my exhaustion.

Beckett plays in my head the second I close my eyes. His cocky smile, his sharp eyes, his rippling muscles, his arm protecting me. And him holding a gun to my head.

He was going to kill me.

He was going to kill me.

He was going to kill me.

I repeat the words over and over. To remind me of the pain of what he did. To remind me that I can't love him. To deepen the knife in my heart.

Tears spill onto the silk pillowcase, escaping my closed eyes.

It hurts, it fucking hurts. And I don't know how to make it stop.

I lie in bed for hours, willing myself to sleep. I try to convince myself I'll feel better in the morning if I can just get some sleep.

But sleep never comes.

Agitated and uncomfortable, I decide to head downstairs to get some food. If I'm lucky, I'll find some alcohol to soothe the ache in my chest and hopefully knock me out to sleep.

I walk into the kitchen and stop when I see a shadow standing in the kitchen. I reach for my gun before realizing I didn't bring one down.

Stupid, stupid.

"Forgot your gun?" Ryker says.

A whoosh of a breath eases out of me when I realize it's Ryker and not an intruder come to kill me.

"You scared the crap out of me." I walk over to where he's standing with a cabinet open over the fridge.

"Sorry. You should always carry a gun with you, Ri. You can never be too careful."

I nod. "I know. Today has just been..." I sigh. "The worst day. I'm not myself. And I'm not thinking straight."

Ryker pulls a bottle down from the cabinet.

"The house came stocked with liquor too?"

"The last owners must have left this bottle of whiskey, but it'll do the trick," he says.

I nod.

I find two glasses, and he pours the amber liquid. We each end up with more than three shots worth in our glass, but I'm still not sure it's going to be enough.

Ryker takes his glass and walks out onto the back deck. I follow him, not sure if he wants to be alone tonight or not. But there's something about being under the dark sky, the bright moon, and chill air that puts everything in perspective in moments like this.

I lean against the railing of the deck as I sip my drink. Ryker does the same.

For a moment, there is just comfortable silence between us as we drink and look up at the sky. All of our answers will be given if we just stand here long enough.

"Today was one of my worst days, but I don't understand why it was one of your worst days, Ri."

I sigh, not sure I want to discuss this with him. "Because today I learned how foolish I had been to give my heart to a man who obliterated it the first chance he got."

"This is Beckett, I assume?"

I nod, almost ashamed.

"Tell me what happened."

I chew on my bottom lip, not sure I want to open my heart to more heartbreak of having to relive it all. But I need to talk to someone, and after what Ryker did today, I trust him a lot more than before.

"Short story is I fell in love with him. I thought he fell in love with me. But in reality, he was just playing me. He thought I was the one responsible for killing his wife. Instead of talking to me about it, he decided to kill me as retribution in front of his people."

My hand shakes as I speak, and I find I'm rattled to my core as I speak the truth of what happened.

Ryker places his hand gently on top of mine, gently calming me with his touch.

"He'll come for me. Tonight. Tomorrow. The next day."

"To finish what he failed to complete?" Ryker asks.

"No. It turns out his wife is alive, so obviously, I didn't kill her. But he'll still come, though."

"What makes you so sure?"

I look at Ryker. "Because he always does."

I lift the glass to my lips and finish the rest of the liquor. It burns going down, making me feel something other than my broken heart for a split second. I wish it would last, but it won't.

I only hope the mixture of exhaustion and alcohol now warming my system will be enough to get me to sleep soon. Sleep is the only way to numb the pain.

Although, I suspect my heartbreak will even seep into my dreams.

Suddenly Ryker speaks. "I'm going to play devil's advocate for a second."

I narrow my eyes. "What do you mean?"

"I think there's a reason Beckett always comes back to you."

I shake my head. "I don't understand. Because he hates me and wants to ruin me?"

Ryker laughs. "Maybe. You know him better than I do, but I'm going to call it something that is very much like hate. As rich and deep as hate, but it isn't."

I glare at him with a deep frown as I pull my hand back from his touch. "Love. You mean love."

He nods slowly, eyeing me skeptically like he thinks I might punch him for even suggesting it.

"It's not love. No one would try to kill someone they loved."

Ryker goes silent, and I realize what I just said.

"I'm sorry—I didn't mean—"

"You did," Ryker cuts me off. "That's okay, but you're wrong. I killed Hector. He was a friend. It wasn't romantic love, but you could say I loved him. Before today I would have said I would give my life to protect him. But then today happened, and I had to make a choice.

"I had to put you and my men above him. He wouldn't have stopped; he would have come after us. I knew his skill; he would have eventually succeeded if I didn't stop him. So I killed someone that I loved."

His words hit me hard. I know the kind of pressure Beckett was under as the new leader of the Retribution Kings. *Did he have to make a similar choice to Ryker? Did he have to choose between two people he loved? Between revenge for Odette and me?*

It doesn't heal my broken heart, but it does put his actions more into perspective.

"What do I do now? How do I get out of this?" I ask Ryker, not really expecting an answer but just needing to say that out loud.

He sighs.

"There isn't any hope that I survive these games and get to choose my own fate, is there? I'm doomed to be married to a horrible man who will rape me and use me as an incubator for his sperm. I'll be disposable as soon as I produce a male heir. That's my future."

"It doesn't have to be."

"No? I don't see a way out of this. Not anymore."

"Yes, you do." Ryker uses a finger to turn my head in his direction, tilting my head up so that our eyes are level with each other. Our lips, our entire bodies, are so close that our breaths are hot on the other's skin.

"You win."

I chuckle. "Not likely. Vincent will never let me win. He'll manipulate the last games to make sure I lose."

"Maybe. Or maybe you find a way to beat him at his own game. You find a way to manipulate him into giving you the advantage, and then you kick all of our asses."

I frown. "Don't you want to win?"

"I want to ensure my men stay alive, that's all."

"But if you lose, that means you've most likely been killed."

"As long as my men are protected, I don't care."

"You're a better man than I realized."

He smiles gently.

"But even if I win, I still have to marry someone. I still

have to produce an heir to take over my father's kingdom. I still—"

"Then you pick the best fucking man. A man you want. A man who will treat you with respect. A man who will love you like you deserve to be loved."

"And you think you're that man?" I exhale, barely able to breathe.

His lips brush mine. It's a soft, sweet, tender kiss. His touch steals my breath and soothes my aching soul—two broken people sharing a healing kiss. The problem is the holes in our hearts are too big to be healed, even by a kiss like this.

He pulls back. "No, I'm not that man. You already know who that man is."

Then Ryker walks back inside, leaving me alone on the deck under the stars with the tingle of his kiss on his lips.

I know exactly who Ryker thinks I should be with, *but why couldn't I have fallen for a man like Ryker?* He's kinder and more self-sacrificing than I realized. He deserves to be a leader in Corsi's kingdom.

Instead, I fell for a man as fucked up as I am. A man who will never admit his feelings for me. A man who threatened to kill me. A man who has saved me more times than I can count. A man who fucking loves me but will put his pride first. A man who chose another woman.

Beckett Monroe.

I look out into the darkness. He won't come tonight. But when he does come, I'm going to be ready to punish him for every transgression he's ever committed against me.

I know my odds aren't great. It's me against a couple dozen men unless Gage, Lennox, and Hayes realize what's happening and decide to fight. But I'm done living my life for others. I'm done living afraid. I'm done hiding my feelings and letting others dictate my future.

For the first time in forever, I know what I want. I realize my mistakes, and I won't be repeating them. And I'd rather go down fighting for what I want than living a lie for another second.

I draw my gun and fire into Stan's leg before anyone realizes what's happening.

Stan curses but doesn't reach for his weapon immediately. He may have been chosen as the number two, but he isn't a skilled fighter. He's young and inexperienced.

It gives me a slight advantage for a second before he starts barking orders. I'm not sure the men even realize what happened at first.

I need to make a run for it. My choices are to dart into the woods or jump in a car and hope I can outdrive them.

Neither are great options, but I have to try. I won't die with Ri not knowing the truth.

I dart into the house, deciding that it gives me some cover until I decide which way to make my exit. Or it becomes my gravesite when they decide to just blow the house up rather than deal with me.

No, they won't do that. Odette is inside; they won't hurt her.

I slam the door shut and close the half dozen locks shut on the door. It will help to keep them out for at least a few minutes.

I consider asking the guys for help, but I won't ask them to betray their own families for me. I'm on my own.

I run out the back, deciding my best bet is to disappear into the woods. Suddenly, Hayes pokes his head out.

"I heard a gunshot," he says.

"I shot Stan."

"Oh." Hayes grabs his gun, and then Lennox is right beside him.

There's a loud bang against the front door.

"Let me go out the back. I'll disappear into the woods. You stay. I won't ask you to betray the oath you took to your families. All I ask is you help me escape the house."

"No," Lennox says, stepping forward.

Gage pops out of the other bedroom and is now looking at me as well.

Fuck, I made a mistake. They are going to turn me over to Stan. I shouldn't have come back into the house.

"We are on your side, not the Retribution Kings. You are our leader. We trust you, not Stan," Lennox says.

"Even if that means you're betraying your people? Betraying everyone you've ever loved? I'm done being a Retribution King. I'm going to be living my life on the run. I refuse to do what they ask of me."

Hayes grins, almost excited by words. "I never liked being a King. I always wanted to be a rebel."

"I'm tired of being lied to. I trust you, not Caius, and not the other Kings," Lennox says with a vengeance in his eyes.

Gage finally chimes in too. "You already know I'm on your side."

I suck in a breath, feeling a heavy weight on my shoulders. It was easier to fight and possibly die when it was just my life on the line. Now it's these three men too, and I'm not sure I made the right decision.

"How do we escape? There are over twenty men outside at Stan's command ready to kill me if I don't finish my initiation task."

"They still want you to kill Ri even after it's obvious she didn't kill Odette?" Hayes asks.

"No, they want me to kill my brother for taking Odette, even though I know that's not what happened."

"Lying bitch," Lennox says.

All eyes turn to him. "I didn't believe one word she said. She's playing us all. She's a Retribution King through and through. She and Caius have set this whole thing up to cause a war."

I nod my agreement. "They chose me as the leader and made me fall in love with Odette, so they could set up my brother in hopes that I would start a war with him. I don't know why they want Enzo dead, but they think since I've worked for him for so long that I know how to defeat him."

Gage curses under his breath.

"We need to get out of here. Should we run into the woods? Find an abandoned house to wait them out or hotwire a car?" I ask, spitballing ideas.

"No, the house is a fortress. Completely bulletproof and bombproof. And they already have the house completely surrounded," Gage says.

"Then what?" I ask.

Hayes grins sadistically. "We pick them off one by one."

Everyone pulls out their guns and nod in agreement. I suspect there is more to each of these guys' stories about why they don't like the Retribution Kings. They so easily believe their former family would betray me.

"Where are Odette and Caius?" I ask.

"Tied up in separate rooms," Lennox answers.

"Then let's do this."

"The glass and walls are bulletproof, so it shouldn't easily shatter, but it will eventually," Gage says.

"What's the plan, then?" Hayes and everyone else look at me.

"Each of us takes a different direction. I'll call everyone on a group call. Keep the line of communication open. If you're wounded or need help, say so. No one plays the hero," I say.

"That includes you," Gage says, narrowing his eyes at me.

I nod.

"I'll take the front," I say.

"I'll take the back," Gage says.

"West," Lennox says at the same time Hayes says, "East."

I pull out my phone and dial them all at the same time. I put my phone on speaker and slide it into my back pocket.

"Can everyone hear me?" I ask.

"Loud and clear," Hayes answers back.

"Yep," Lennox and Gage answer.

I raise my gun as I lean against the frame of the front window and peer outside from the corner of my eye.

I don't see Stan anywhere, but I do see at least five men trying to break down the front door.

One of my guys starts shooting. There is no going back now.

I slip the window open wide enough for me to shoot through the space, and then I fire as well.

I hit the first attacker easily enough, and he drops to the ground. The others return fire, but I don't back down. Gage said the glass is bulletproof; it's time to find out.

I keep shooting but refuse to duck as the bullets fly at me. I can't help but flinch as they hit the window next to me that shatters slightly but doesn't break.

I exhale a deep breath.

"Everyone good?" I ask.

Three *good*s ring back at me.

I grin, believing for the first time that we are going to win this fight and win big. Then it will only be a matter of finding Ri and figuring out a way to not have a dozen gangs after us.

It takes about five minutes for me to kill the rest on my side of the house.

I still hear gunfire ringing out.

"The front is clear. Who needs help?"

But before I can move, I get all clears from everyone else.

"Meet in the living room," I say.

When I see everyone walk in unscathed, I relax.

"They were idiots for attacking the house when they

knew how protected it was," Hayes says as he falls into a chair.

Lennox and Gage sit on the couch while I stand in front of the fireplace.

"Did anyone kill Stan?" I ask.

Everyone shakes their heads no.

I run my hand through my hair. "Fuck, he must have escaped. The slick bastard wouldn't even stay and fight."

"But he will bring more men. He'll come after you and threaten everything you care about unless you do as they want. You'll never be safe again," Lennox says.

"We'll never be safe again. Are you sure you guys are ready for that life?" I ask.

"We're with you," Gage says as the others nod.

"What do we do now?" Hayes asks.

"We find Ri, and then we find a way to win the game and end the Retribution Kings."

Silence stretches around the room as the guys exchange glances.

"What?" I ask.

Hayes scratches his head and then finally speaks. "Ri hates your guts."

I chuckle as the guys stare at me like I've lost my mind.

"I know she hates me."

"If you go see her now, she's going to kick your ass. And she's way better skilled than those guys we just fought."

"I know. She hates me, and it's well deserved, but I have to go see her. I have to fix things," I say.

Hayes smirks. "I'm going to enjoy watching her beat you up."

The others chuckle.

"If she beats me up, that means she'll see me. I'll

accept whatever punishment she needs to inflict; I just need to see her."

"This is going to end badly. She really hates you right now," Hayes says.

"She also loves me," I say.

No one argues with that.

8

———

RI

Two days pass.

No one attacks us.

No one comes looking for us.

I'm almost impressed by Ryker's ability to find a safe house that no one has actually found.

Lucy has been going stir crazy in the house. She's an extrovert who likes to be busy. She likes school, work, and being around people. Unfortunately for her, Ryker and I haven't been the best company these days.

Ryker and I have been enjoying the peace and quiet. Neither of us is used to getting a quiet moment to think. And every night, we have met out on the back deck and talked when we couldn't sleep.

He told me about past loves. About what taking on a leadership position meant. About what he wants for the future.

I tried everything to not talk about Beckett, but in reality, it was all I talked about. It's all I've thought about. *Why hasn't he come?*

I thought he would at least come to finish what he started. I'm definitely not expecting an apology.

He's forgotten all about me now that Odette is back. He's probably fucking her brains out and hasn't given me a thought.

He loves her, not me.

I'm so stupid, so foolish.

"Stop it," Ryker says as we once again stand under the moonlight.

"Stop what?" I ask as I drink my midnight whiskey.

"Stop beating yourself up. It's not your fault you fell in love with him. It's his fault he hurt and betrayed you. You did nothing wrong. Loving someone is never foolish, even if they didn't deserve it. Falling in love with him shows how big of a heart you have. You're incredible to love someone with so many faults. You saw the best in him, and there is nothing wrong with finding the best in others."

I sigh. "But is it foolish to keep loving him?"

Ryker sighs as he tucks a strand of my hair behind my ear. His touch sends chills through my body.

I lean into him, and then our arms are wrapped around each other. We comfort each other the only way we know how, but it's not enough. Hugging each other is nice, but we would both rather be hugging other people. This is all we've got, though.

A throat clears, and Ryker pushes my body behind his. We both drop our glasses and draw our guns, aiming into the darkness of the forest beyond the deck. I try to move out from behind Ryker, but he holds me steadily behind him.

"Who's there?" I ask.

There is no answer, but a chill creeps over me. I instinctively know who it is.

"It's okay," I whisper in Ryker's ear.

He leans his head in my direction, and I can see the yearning in his eyes. He wishes I wasn't fine. He wishes he could protect me. He wishes I wouldn't say it's okay for Beckett to come back into my life.

I'm not saying any of those things, though. I'm not letting Beckett back into my life. I'm just saying I won't let him hurt me again. He can't hurt me again. I won't let him. But I plan on hurting him plenty for what he did to me.

Slowly I move out from behind Ryker. He tenses, the muscles in his back rippling to hold me back, but I gently shake my head and step around him. I'm not going to face Beckett again while ducking behind another man. I'm going to face him face to face.

"You going to show yourself? Or hide in the shadows like a coward?" I ask, my voice full of sass.

Chuckles ring out, but they don't belong to Beckett.

I smirk as I see Hayes, Gage, and Lennox step into the light from the deck.

"You might want to put the gun down, Princess, if you expect Beckett to show his face. We all know your motto of shooting first and asking questions later. We all know you'll shoot his balls off," Hayes teases, walking up the deck like he's my best friend.

He comes in for a hug, and I let him wrap around me. I relish his touch. I've forgotten how much I consider them friends.

"And he would deserve it," I say.

Hayes shrugs. "Yea, but then you'd be sad because you still secretly want his cock."

I growl.

Hayes laughs and then lounges on one of the chairs on the deck like he's ready to watch a good show.

Lennox greets me next. "Give him hell, Princess," he whispers into my ear when he hugs me.

I nod.

Lastly, Gage embraces me. "But not too much hell, Princess. He has a story to tell, as I suspect you do too. That story might change your heart quite a bit."

I frown.

"Why do you let them call you Princess, but I can't?" Ryker asks.

"There's no controlling these dogs," I say with a huff.

"That, and we have an intimate relationship with Princess," Hayes says.

I roll my eyes. He's just trying to get Beckett riled up.

Ryker tilts his head and raises his dark eyebrows at me.

I shrug. "I've fucked them. Actually, I fucked them all at the same time." I grin brightly, not ashamed of it in the least. It was still one of the most erotic moments of my life if you exclude my experiences with Beckett. And I do—I want to forget all my times with Beckett.

"We'd be happy to repeat the performance, Princess," Hayes says.

I glance over to see Lennox and Gage looking at me with heat in their eyes. My core heats at the thought. It's probably exactly what I need to get over Beckett.

Instead, I turn and look out into the darkness. "Still a coward, I see."

After a beat, I see his shadow move.

My throat tightens up, and every emotion possible overtakes me when I see him. I avoid his eyes, not wanting to see how he feels when he looks at me. Instead, I examine the rest of him.

His jeans hug his thick muscular legs. His black shirt is tight against his body, but I can't tell if there is any blood or dirt on it. I suspect that's why he is almost always wearing dark shirts. There is no gun or weapon in his hand. He stands like an easy target in front of me. Oh, how easy it would be to shoot him in the balls as Hayes said.

I smile at that thought, even though I won't.

Actually, I might.

But then I look at his face. The hardness, the sadness, the emptiness. The look of longing, and want, and desire. It's all there in his brown pupils. He doesn't have to say a word for me to see his pain. He doesn't have to move a muscle. I know.

Then why?

Why?

Why?

Why?

Why did you try to kill me?

Why did you go back to her?

Why did you choose her over me?

And why come back to hurt me all over again?

I tear my eyes from him and look at the others.

"Where are Caius and Odette?"

Lennox snickers. "We left them tied up in the cabin by the lake."

My eyes widen. "What? Why?"

"That's what happens when you lie to everyone," Gage responds.

I frown, completely confused.

I look over to Beckett to see if his face will confirm or deny the facts. His expression doesn't change. He just stares at me like I'm breath itself.

It doesn't change anything, even if it's true. I don't

understand what Caius and Odette did to piss them off, but I suspect they are safe. Beckett might be pissed with his wife for running all this time, but she had her reasons —reasons I can understand better than anyone.

Ryker is still gripping his gun, but it's now aimed down at his side. He's ready to step in if I need him.

My gun, on the other hand, is aimed at Beckett. He doesn't flinch when I move the gun. In fact, I'd say his sad eyes are begging me to shoot him to put him out of his misery. That would be too easy, though.

"What are you doing here, Beckett?" I ask, lowering my gun and putting it into the back of my joggers.

If I spill any of his blood, it will be with my bare hands, not a gun.

He doesn't answer me. He just looks at me, and I swear he's holding his breath. There is no smart comment. No 'I'm here to beg for forgiveness.' No 'can we talk in private away from all of these guys.' Nothing.

I bite my bottom lip down so hard in frustration I swear I draw blood.

"Did you lose your vocal cords in a fight, or are you just not going to talk to me?"

Beckett is silent.

I don't know what game he's playing, but it appears he isn't going to talk to me.

Fine.

If he wants to act childish, then fucking fine.

I don't know what he's doing here if he won't talk to me.

I turn toward the guys, hoping they have answers.

Gage is frowning at Beckett.

Lennox rolls his eyes with a soft smile.

Hayes has a shit-eating grin on his face.

And Ryker looks as lost as I am.

I have no idea what to do.

But I have so much pent-up anger inside, so much rage. And my chest—every pump of my heart fills it with pain, and it's all because of him.

"You were going to kill me," I say, my voice shaky and my palms sweaty. "You were going to shoot me in the head in front of everyone." My voice is stronger this time.

I turn back and look full on at Beckett. His hand is in his pocket, and he doesn't flinch at my words. His lips don't part to argue back, so I continue.

"You manipulated me, played me because you thought you could pull a confession out of me. You thought I was responsible for your *wife's* death."

I take a deep breath. "All you had to do to find out the truth was ask. You could have shown me the fucking evidence and seen if I could have explained what the hell happened."

I feel a tear in the corner of my eye, but I don't let it out. I refuse to show him how much he hurt me.

"Odette is alive. I didn't kill her. In fact, I helped her. I'm sorry that by helping her, I hurt you. But if you truly love her, you can't blame her for doing what was best for her. And you can't blame me for helping the woman you love," my voice cracks.

I can see the guys out of the corner of my eye stare at me in confusion. But this speech isn't for them; it's for Beckett.

"And yet, you come here and don't apologize. You don't even have the balls to speak to me. I hate you! I fucking hate you." My tear slips out, dammit.

I'm out of breath.

I'm exhausted from not sleeping well.

And I hate myself as much as I hate him.

Because I still love the bastard.

He's not mine, he's hers, but I still love him. I want the best for him. I couldn't shoot him even if I wanted to.

I have to stop loving him.

He's not mine.

He never will be.

It's not going to be easy, but I have to start the process of healing. There is only one way to stop the bleeding.

I turn to Ryker, who is looking at me with sad puppy dog eyes. I grab the back of his neck and jerk his lips to mine. It's a harsh, messy kiss. Our lips barely meet. I'm kissing his cheek as much as I am his lips, but I don't care.

Beckett probably thinks I'm doing this as revenge or punishment for what he did to me. But this is all for me.

I need to move on from Beckett.

I need to stop thinking about him every second of every day. Stop pining for him. Stop believing in the fairy-tale that one of us will win the games, and we will live happily ever after together.

We are nothing but toxic destruction to each other. He may not have a heart that he ever gave me, but mine is demolished, broken beyond repair. It may never work properly again, but I have to try. I deserve to try. I deserve to be happy. I deserve so much more.

This kiss is the start of that recovery.

I need a night to forget about Beckett. A night to feel alive again. A night to hope.

I expect Ryker to pull away. He's already kissed me and told me he isn't the man for me.

He doesn't pull away, though.

Beckett doesn't attack us or say anything.

The other guys just watch intently like they wish they were the ones being kissed.

Ryker grabs the back of my neck and tilts me back as his tongue slips roughly inside mine. It's hot and thick in my mouth and not a bit gentle.

Thank heavens for that. I don't need gentle. I need rough animal sex to make me forget. I need to forget the man standing not twenty feet from me that I thought was the one I've been looking for my entire life.

Ryker's other hand moves to my hip as he pulls me roughly against him. My breath catches in my throat as he begins moving his hand up from my waist to underneath the hem of my shirt.

His thumb strokes my bare stomach, and I shiver. I move to pull away, thoughts of why I shouldn't do this starting to sneak in, but he sucks on my bottom lip, sending an unending wave of pleasure through my body, and I no longer want to disengage.

As great as Ryker is, though, he's not enough. Not nearly enough.

Not when Beckett is right there.

Not when I want to run to him and tear his clothes off and attack him. I don't care that he's married. I don't care that he loves another woman. I don't—

Fuck, I have to stop.

I grab the neck of Ryker's shirt as I start guiding us backward.

I will not look at Beckett.

I will pretend he doesn't exist.

I will think of all the other hot guys on this deck.

I will think of all the other incredible guys in the world.

That's my mantra as Ryker and I walk to the center of

the three other guys who have been watching us kiss wordlessly.

I pull my lips off Ryker. He protests, trying to pull my lips back against his, but I hold up one finger to his lips. Then I turn a heated gaze on the three guys sitting on the deck.

I don't say a word, but they all know what I'm asking— the same thing I asked of them before.

The reasoning this time is different. Last time it was about defying my father and giving myself control. This time it's about moving on, but both times are about saving myself.

I turn my attention back to Ryker as I kiss him once again. I'm not sure if any of the guys are going to answer my request. They have their boss to consider this time. I gave them all an open invitation, but it's up to them.

Hayes is the first to accept my invitation. He gets up from his seat and comes up behind me, sweeping my hair off the back of my neck and kissing me in the nook at the base of my neck.

I gasp as shockwaves burst through me.

I see Ryker eye Hayes, and for a moment, I think Ryker might protest sharing me. If he does, he can leave. This is about me and my needs. If he isn't up for sharing, then he can suffer alone.

Ryker doesn't say anything or seem upset as he nibbles back on my bottom lip. Suddenly he spins me around until I'm facing Hayes.

Hayes grins down at me. "I always knew someday you'd ask for seconds." Quickly his lips crash down on mine. He tastes like bubblegum and smells like citrus. He kisses lazily like he knows he doesn't have to try hard to get my panties wet. And he doesn't. His kisses are fantastic

—just enough tongue, just enough pressure, just about enough.

Ryker takes Hayes's former spot behind me until I'm trapped between two hard bodies. Ryker nibbles on my earlobe, and I buck as his teeth scrape.

Jesus, they're going to kill me. What did I get myself into?

I want to glance over at Beckett to see what he's doing. I'm about to break away and do just that when Lennox stands, blocking any view I would have had.

His eyes glaze with need as he walks toward me with a serious expression. Before he even gets to me, Hayes has spun me towards Lennox. Lennox catches me and dips me back as his lips take a turn with my mouth. His might be the most aggressive kiss of any of them so far. It takes my breath away, and I barely have a chance to breathe in his scent. It's musky and manly, and just how I knew he'd smell.

Lennox lifts me back up and spins me back around. His hand palms my breast as I arch into him.

"Take it back. Take it all back. Your pride. Your strength. Your heart. Take it all back, Princess," he demands into my ear.

I purse my lips, barely able to breathe, before Gage steps in front of me and demands his turn. His kiss is the softest and most tender. His kiss gives me time to breathe, but not enough to think.

Then Gage takes my hand and leads me forward. I look down and see the others have pulled a coffee table from inside out onto the deck. They've laid a thick blanket and pillow on top.

I bite on my bottom lip as I stare at the scene in front of me. Thoughts of the last time I let four men have their way with me rush through my head.

Gage releases my hand and puts his hands in his pockets as he watches me make my decision. They all do. Hayes is the only one who raises an eyebrow in challenge.

I smirk at him, knowing this is how I take my heart back. I fuck them—all of them.

They are all great guys, but I probably won't fall in love with any of them. I'm not sure any of them would want me to anyway. Next time I fall in love, I won't fall easily. But this isn't about falling in love. This is about taking back my heart.

I take a step toward the coffee table and then lie down on my back on top of the blanket and pillow. My heart is beating a million miles a minute, my breath is too fast, and I'm sure they all think I'll back out at any second. But I won't, I need this.

Then I make a conscious decision—one for my benefit, not his. I look at Beckett and take back my heart.

9

———

BECKETT

I DON'T SPEAK when I see Ri.

I thought I'd have an endless stream of words to say. I thought I'd apologize, be down on my knees begging for forgiveness. I thought I'd try explaining the truth of what happened. I would explain, show her the video, beg, and plead.

I'd tell her how I feel about her.

I'd tell her that I love her, not Odette. Not any other woman—her. It's always been her. I've never loved like I love her. She's my equal in every way.

And then I saw Ri. I saw her standing next to Ryker. I saw her, and I knew that I had no right to speak. No right to beg for forgiveness. No right to plead down on my knees.

Ri had every right to her anger.

Every right to want to murder me for what she thinks I've done.

And any words I said wouldn't matter. Not until she got out what she needed to say, so I gave her the floor. I let her speak. If I had even said one word, I wouldn't have been able to stop myself from crumbling to the ground in apology. So I kept silent.

Listening to her words was torture. I could feel her pain with every syllable.

I stood still, knowing if I moved I'd break. My heart was just as broken as hers, but I'm not as strong, not nearly as strong as her.

She doesn't realize it—that she holds my heart in her hands, but she will. She'll stab it the first chance she gets, but I don't care. As long as she realizes it's hers, and it will always be hers.

So I keep silent.

I just watch and endure.

And endure I do because Ri doesn't stop at just yelling at me. No, she has to punish me even further by kissing Ryker. And Hayes, and Lennox, and Gage...

Every kiss is a bullet through my heart. I have no idea how I'm still standing, still breathing, still fucking alive. Probably because Ri deserves to torture me until my very last breath.

But then she does something I know I won't survive. She lies down on the coffee table in the middle of four horny assholes, laying her body out for them to do what they want with it.

Fucking hell.

Someone just shot me now. My fist twitches wanting to go punch every single man surrounding her. Most are supposed to be my friends, only one my enemy. But some friends they are if they are willingly kissing and touching what's mine.

They know how I feel, and they are still going to do this. If I somehow survive this, I'm going to kill them all for this.

And then Ri looks at me, the first time since she started kissing Ryker. There's a change in her eyes. This isn't about me. This isn't about punishing me. This is about her.

About her needs.

Her taking back control.

Her finding her strength.

Her becoming whole again.

My chest tightens at the sight—how fucking incredible a sight it is. My eyes widen in wonder as I look at her. Ri isn't one to back down in defeat. She always rises back up —always.

I will too.

If I'm her equal, I have to become stronger. I have to stop putting my feelings above hers. I have to become more.

I wish I could give her an encouraging word, a smile, something that shows that I'm not only okay with her doing this, but I encourage it. All I can muster is a solemn nod.

I'm not as strong as you, Fighter, but I will be. I'll have to be.

Then she looks back at Hayes, who is standing between her legs. Ryker is on one side, Lennox on the other, and Gage is by her head.

I can do this. I can do this. I can do this.

Gage kisses her upside down as Ryker and Lennox each palm a breast. Hayes kisses over her pants between her legs.

Fuck, I can't do this.

I'm sweating and jittery and want to disappear into a puddle on the floor rather than watch this.

But then Ri lets out a throaty moan. For some reason,

that single syllable calms me. It also stirs my dick, but it washes through me like a warm drink.

Ri needs this to reclaim herself.

I can't give her what she needs right now, but they can.

Ryker lifts her shirt up, exposing her tight abs. He kneels next to her and kisses each rippling muscle, worshipping her body like she deserves. Now I realize my role—ensure they treat her right. Treat her better than I ever have. If they hurt her, I'll step in. Otherwise, I'll watch from the darkness.

Gage lifts her shirt all the way off.

Silence stretches as all the men admire her bare torso. She's not wearing a bra; all that remains is her pajama pants.

I can barely see her body from my angle, but it's enough for me to vow I'll never hurt her ever fucking again. I'd say she looks like an angel, but I know she's anything but an angel. She's a skilled warrior capable of defending herself against anything.

Lennox and Ryker take no time devouring her nipples with their mouths. Her back arches into them, and soft moans are pulled from her lips. Gage lets a few escape before he plants his lips over her mouth, muffling the sound a little.

Hayes continues to kiss gently over her pants but doesn't move to take them off.

I focus on her eyes. They come alive with each kiss and touch of one of the men. She doesn't look at me, and I don't expect her to. This is about her, not me, but damn do I want her to look at me. Selfishly, I want to see the full pleasure she's feeling reflected in her eyes.

She hasn't had much pleasure in her life, so I'm

grateful for every drop of it she'll experience, even if it's not me giving it to her.

"Please," I hear her beg. "Please, I need more."

Her eyes are locked on Hayes, who chuckles back at her.

"So needy, Princess," he responds, hooking his fingers under the waistband of her pants and then pulling, yanking them off her body in one fluid motion. And then she's completely bare to them.

Her skin glows under the moonlight, and I'm thankful for how private this backyard is. I can barely stand that these four men get to see her body.

She's not yours. She can do what she likes with her body.

I just hope someday I'm worthy of her again. Even if I hadn't royally fucked everything up, I'm still not sure I would be worthy, but I'm going to try every day.

Hayes kneels between her legs, and every other man's movement slows, letting her focus all of her attention on him. Their eyes lock, and they both lick their lips at the same time. Her chest rises and falls, and I swear his does too at the same time. They are perfectly in sync. He knows exactly what she needs.

He lowers his head between her legs, never losing eye contact with her. He's giving her complete control. Just before his tongue reaches that apex between her legs, she nods slightly, giving him all the permission he needs.

He licks up her slit, so slowly I think it's going to take all night. At that moment, there's a connection that beams off of Ri. It's like she's connected to all of us at that moment. We'd all do anything for her. She has that effect on men. It could be why so many of us want her, will fight to the death for her.

But I'm the only one willing to give my soul up to her. I'm not touching her, not kissing her like the others, but I know the moment she feels my vow hit her through the darkness in a delicious shiver up her spine.

I vow to love you forever.

I vow to be worthy.

I vow to give you my heart and soul.

Even if you don't choose me, I'm yours.

She doesn't have to look at me to know she feels it. She closes her eyes as the guys devour her, just enjoying the moment.

She reaches out to them, trying to touch them, to undo their pants, to give them a little of the pleasure they are giving to her.

Each of them slowly swats her hand away, kissing her palms, stopping her from touching them. This isn't about them—this is all her. That or they think I'll murder them if they sink their dicks into her.

Hayes slips two fingers inside her, his tongue flicking over her clit.

Come, baby, come for them. Take back your heart, your strength, your everything. Take my heart, my soul, my very existence along with it.

She bites her lip as she writhes between their touches. Her body shakes slightly, but she doesn't come yet. They all intensify their actions. They stroke her faster, suck her harder. She's close but not there yet.

With one word, I could make her come at this moment, but she has to find it herself. She has to let go of all the pain I and every other man in her life have caused her and take herself back.

She needs to recapture every bit of control and every bit of who she is.

She inches closer but still doesn't come.

The guys try harder, but it's not about what they are doing—it's about her. She's the only one who can control if she can come or not.

Come, Fighter.

Then, almost as if she'd been holding back to spite them all, she glances my way, and I see sharp daggers in her eyes a second before she looks up at the sky. Like the goddess she is, she explodes like a shooting star across the sky.

The sound she makes vibrates through the night air and shoots through my chest. It breaks me and heals me at the same time. Her sound is pure hell and heaven. It's every emotion she's ever felt wrapped up in one sound.

The guys step back from her as she comes. None of them can take their eyes off of her. They all just watch incredulously at the woman they just worshipped. A woman who should be broke and battered just reclaimed her power.

Everyone is silent, not sure what to do next. Ri stands, not the least bit concerned with her nakedness. She struts inside the house with all of us drooling after her.

We all stare for a moment, and then Ryker breaks the silence. "Damn man, how were you ever foolish enough to hurt that woman?"

I sigh. "Because I'm a fucking idiot."

10

RI

I FELT like a goddess coming under the moonlight and stars. It felt freeing to be touched by four guys at once without them wanting anything in return from me. If I'm not careful, I'm not going to be able to come without multiple men worshipping me.

I chuckle.

I've only made it just inside the house. The lights are off inside, so they can't see me. I touch my bottom lip as I think about what I just did.

Again.

This is the second time I've had multiple guys fuck me at once.

And yet, all I want is one.

I take a deep breath, my lungs rising and slamming down in my ribcage. I feel better than I have in days. From the orgasm, from making Beckett watch, from making him suffer. He may not love me, but he definitely didn't like me shoving that in his face.

I'm not healed. I'm not magically fixed, but damn do I feel better—stronger and in more control.

I watch the guys for a second longer before I head up the stairs. I fall into bed, not bothering to shower or wipe their scent off of me. I just collapse and sleep for the first time in days.

———

I wake up to see it's still pitch-black outside—so much for a long, refreshing sleep.

I sigh and pad to the bathroom to pee, hoping I'll be able to fall back asleep afterward. The second my feet hit the ground, though, I realize my waking has nothing to do with a full bladder. I have unfinished business with a certain someone, and it needs finishing—now.

I wrap a robe from the closet around me, put my gun in the pocket, and then head downstairs. It's early in the morning, but I might as well make myself a cup of coffee to wait for him to wake up.

I make it down the stairs, and the hairs on my arms stiffen—Beckett's awake.

I consider running back upstairs and pretending to sleep, but I won't cower. I need to face him. I got my strength back; now I have to deal with reality. I'm sure he came here for answers, needing them as badly as I do.

He wants to know why I helped Odette, why I lied to him. I need to know why he was going to kill me, but not after taking my heart and soul and everything I am. He could have just killed me without making me fall for him.

I walk to the kitchen and see him sitting with his back to me at the circular table, staring out the back window. His back straightens when he hears my footsteps and feels that it's me.

He doesn't say anything.

Neither do I.

I walk to the kitchen to make a pot of coffee, not because I really want the caffeine, but just to have something to fidget with before talking to him. Once I hear him say he loves Odette, his wife, I'll crumple—not fully, not all the way again, but it will be hard to hear that he'll forever be out of my life.

I get to the coffee maker and see a pot already made.

I sigh—so much for that plan. I pour myself a cup and turn to face the man I will probably always love.

He doesn't turn around. He lets me come to him.

I take a seat opposite him, staring down at my coffee. After a few breaths, I finally look up.

He looks broken but not as shattered as I'd hoped. His eyes are puffy; his entire face looks swollen like he hasn't slept in weeks. His hair is disheveled, and his clothes are wrinkly, like he hasn't changed in days. Somehow, he's still the best-looking guy I've ever seen.

Earlier, he didn't talk, but I have no doubt he will now. He was letting me get everything off my chest before, and he knew there was no use talking to me until I had gotten out every emotion I was harboring.

Now that I did, and we're alone, he'll talk. Somehow that makes me more nervous. My hands begin trembling around the coffee mug.

"Why are you here?" I finally get out. I need to hear him talk. I need to hear that he loves her, that it has always been her.

The croak that initially leaves his throat is my first clue that he's as anxious as me. "I'm not sure you're ready to hear the answer to that question yet."

I frown. "I wouldn't have asked if I wasn't ready to hear it," I snap.

"Well, I guess I'm not ready to answer it yet."

I shake my head; maybe we aren't going to be civil. "You made me fall in love with you. You took my heart, my soul, fucking everything. And then you dragged me in front of the Retribution Kings, tied me to a pole, and were about to shoot me for a crime I didn't commit. You didn't once ask me about what you found. Didn't give me a chance to explain myself. Didn't give me a chance to tell you that I was helping Odette, that I saved her. Your plan was always to kill me in front of everyone, regardless of what I did or said." I catch my breath and glare at him. "You could have just killed me; you didn't have to be so cruel as to make me love you first."

"You love me?"

I roll my eyes. "Not really the point." I'm not about to tell him flat out that I love him to his face, not after what he did.

He rubs his head, the muscles in his bicep flexing.

"Tell me," he says.

"What?"

"Tell me what I didn't give you the chance to say before. Tell me what you did for Odette."

He doesn't deserve an explanation, but I want to get everything off my chest and be done with him after this conversation.

"I was running from a man named Kek."

Beckett doesn't react. I assume he'll yell at me for not telling him who my stalker was earlier when I knew his name, but he doesn't. His face remains neutral and impassive, so I clarify. "Kek is the man who has been stalking me."

He nods slowly but doesn't say anything. No veins

bulge on his head; his cheeks don't turn red; he just waits patiently for me to continue.

Huh?

"Vincent hired Kek to be my bodyguard and companion. He wasn't much older than me, so Vincent thought we would get along."

Beckett doesn't ask any questions. He's completely patient, giving me the floor. It feels strange, almost like I'm telling the story to myself.

"At first, Kek did his job. He helped Vincent train me on how to defend myself, how to wield a gun. He and Vincent taught me everything I know." I swallow down the part of me that feels grateful to two men who helped give me the skills to protect myself while also offering me up as a complete sacrifice.

"Kek came up with this idea one day to help protect me. He thought that if I could self-hypnotize, then even if the worst happened and I was kidnapped and tortured, at least I could be ordered to forget the pain."

Beckett's eyes widen, and his nostrils flare at that, but he still doesn't speak.

"So for years, he worked on that with me. He helped me learn how to hypnotize myself, to help me forget things in case I needed to for my own sanity. It worked. In order for my mind to forget, all I need is a single phrase whispered in my ear."

Beckett leans in.

"No, I'm not going to tell you that phrase."

He smirks and shakes his head.

"But somewhere along the line, Kek no longer became my friend or protector. Maybe he never was. I was too young to do much about him at first. But eventually, Vincent realized Kek's intentions had changed and fired him. He would have killed him, but he vanished, and that was good enough for Vincent."

Beckett's throat bobs up and down, and I can see the question in his eyes.

"Ask me," I say, knowing what he wants to ask.

"Did he—did he rape you? Abuse you?"

"Not in that way, no. But he did hurt me."

The veins in Beckett's arms pop as his hand fists. I can feel rage rippling off him.

"I was running from Kek the day of your wedding. He's the one man who scares me. He's the one man who knows the phrase that can control my mind, make me forget. He knows my physical skills—my strengths and weaknesses. As much as I want to face him, I can't. So I ran and ended up crashing your wedding." I wince. "Sorry about that."

He shakes his head. "Don't be."

"That night, I was hiding in the hotel when I ran into Odette during the reception. I saw terror and fear in her eyes. I didn't know who she was running from, but I knew it was the same fear I was harboring. I told her I'd help her, so I did."

I meet Beckett's gaze, unsure of how he's going to react. He looks heartbroken. I may have helped Odette, but I also caused him so much pain while he endured her being gone, thinking she would never come back.

My own chest tightens, thinking about the suffering he went through. It's the same heartbreak I feel now. He must have felt so betrayed.

He deserves to hear the rest.

"I hid in your hotel suite, hoping to god I wouldn't have to hear any newlywed sex." I wince, remembering them coming into the room. The sounds of their laughs, their kisses—they sounded so fucking happy. My heart swelled listening while also feeling like I was invading a very private moment.

"And then you left to go get her bag. We had limited time before we knew you'd return. We knew there was a video camera, so we had to make it look real while also not seriously hurting Odette so she could run."

I close my eyes, remembering it all clearly now.

"I used a knife. I sliced her skin. Her screams were real. I hated hurting her, but it was the only way. She had a bag of her blood I burst against her chest. That's where most of the blood came from, not from any real wound I inflicted.

"I tied her up, and then she had me call a number for her. I don't know who the men were that helped her escape, but my job was done. Before I left, I knew I could offer her one last thing. I wasn't sure what my future held. I knew that the same dangerous people that were after me could have been after her. If they caught me, I might tell them the truth about Odette—that she wasn't dead."

My throat closes up, thinking about how desperate Odette was at that moment. "So I told Odette my greatest secret."

Beckett leans so far forward in his chair over the table that he might as well be sitting directly in front of me with no table in front of us. He holds his breath as he waits.

"I told her the phrase that would make me forget. She used it. I forgot. Then I ran into Kek in the hallway. His knife cut into my skin, mixing Odette's blood with my own. Helping her almost got me caught, but my adrenaline must have been high because I fought him off and got to the elevator before he could follow me. That's when I ran into you."

We stare at each other across the empty table, lost in

each others' eyes, knowing this might be the last time we sit like this. I don't know if his feelings were ever real toward me, but mine certainly were.

This is the last time I'll let myself feel any glimmer of love for him. After today, I'll lock it all away. When I hear about him and Odette living happily ever after, I won't secretly be pining for him from a distance.

I beg Beckett to speak first. I'm not sure I can say another word. I'm not sure I can bear my heart for much longer. He needs to say his peace. He needs to finish breaking my heart. And then he needs to leave me, forever.

"Please," I whisper so quietly I'm not sure he can hear me. There's a tear at the corner of my eye, but I refuse to release it until he's gone.

Beckett takes a long time to respond, his face looking like he's about to shatter right along with me. He opens his mouth and closes it so many times that he begins to look like a fish to me. It slightly lifts my mood.

Finally, he says, "I don't love Odette."

LISTENING to Ri's truth broke me. She's so selfless, so strong, so determined. I don't know how it was possible for me not to fall in love with her for so long. I don't know how I could have ever loved anyone else.

It's why there's a damn competition to win her. Men want her not just because they get her father's kingdom but because they get her—a strong, fearless fighter. A woman that looks like a princess and fights like a warrior. She's everything I've wanted and everything I never knew I wanted.

I hate myself for making her feel like I didn't love her, like I'd ever choose another.

"I think I just had a hallucination. Can you repeat what you said?" Ri asks.

I sigh.

She's not going to believe me, just like I don't believe Odette. Ri's story matches Odette's, but I know I'm still missing a piece of the puzzle. I need to talk to my brother. I need to figure out the truth, but I need Ri more.

"I don't love Odette," I repeat firmly, so there is no mistaking my words.

Ri blinks, her only reaction.

"I don't know if my marriage to Odette is still legal, but if it is, I'm filing for divorce today."

Another blink.

"I don't believe Odette's story, not fully. I can fill you in later on the rest of the details she shared with me, but I don't believe her."

Double blink.

"I believe you, Ri, every word."

Her mouth falls open, but then she snaps it shut. Two more times, she repeats the action until she's starting to look like a shocked fish.

I smile at her.

"Ask me again."

Color seems to return to her face, and her eyes water.

"Ask me again," I repeat.

She clears her throat. "Why are you here?"

"I'm here to win you back."

"You tried to kill me. I'm not sure you can win me back."

"Except I didn't. I didn't try to kill you."

She crosses her arms across her chest, and her face turns defensive. "You most certainly did. You dragged me into that arena. You tied me to a pole, showed the evidence on the big screen, and then you aimed a gun at my head."

"I didn't." I rub the back of my neck, knowing she won't believe me, but I have to try. I'll keep trying every day until she does finally believe me.

She racks her memory, trying to remember that night. I'm sure most of her memories are foggy after whatever that bastard Kek did to her mind, so I explain as simply as I can.

"In order to become the leader of the Retribution Kings, I was given a final task—get retribution for Odette. Everyone has to get retribution in order to join. It's the final act of initiation."

I bite my tongue, not wanting to say the next part. This is going to get worse before I can make it better.

"The task wasn't a problem at first. I assumed it was your father; everyone did. That is until I found the video of you."

"The video that didn't show the whole truth and that you never once showed to me or asked me about?"

I nod slowly at her anger. "Yes, at first, I thought it was true. I was angry. I wanted to end your life then and there for what you did, but then I studied the video more. If you had wanted Odette dead, you would have ended her life swiftly. She was no match for you. The fight was long and drawn out, and all of her wounds were superficial, not enough to cause the amount of blood we found."

She frowns, her eyes narrowing at me, not understanding what I'm saying.

"So I had Gage dig deeper. He found the truth, but by then, it was too late. I was out of time."

"How were you out of time?"

"If I didn't complete my final initiation task, they would kill me."

She gasps. She cares about me far more than I deserve.

"The problem was I didn't have much proof other than my gut. What Gage found wasn't enough to prove to the room full of people that you didn't hurt Odette, not when Caius was filling their heads with lies."

"I'm confused. You tied me to that pole. You were going to kill me even knowing that I didn't kill Odette?"

"No," I say firmly.

"No?"

"No, I had a plan. Gage, Hayes, and Lennox. I brought you there, knowing Odette would show herself. Gage tracked her to town. The plan was to play on Odette's emotions. I figured Odette would still have feelings for me, and she wouldn't let me die."

Ri frowns, still not understanding.

"When it came time, I turned the gun on myself since they were going to kill me anyway. I was never going to shoot you, though. And I figured if I threatened my own life, Odette would show herself. I was right."

Ri's eyes are big, and her breath is finally calm. "And if you were wrong?" she whispers.

"Then I would have shot myself. The guys knew their job was to get you out of there and take you wherever you wanted to go. They were to help you run, to get free."

"But..." She bites her lip and tucks the robe tighter around her body. "But you'd be dead?"

I nod. "Better than you being dead."

She blinks rapidly, trying to process everything I just said. I didn't try to kill her; I saved her. I don't love Odette.

"This can't be the truth," Ri whispers.

"It is." I want to say more—how much I love her, how much it's her that I want, that I would die for—only her.

I'm not sure she's ready to hear that yet. I'm not even sure she believes me or even can.

Then she looks up, and I see tears spilling down her cheeks.

I frown, not understanding why she's crying. I can't stand the distance anymore, though, so I jump out of my seat and run around the table to her. I yank her chair back and kneel between her legs. Looking up at her, I watch tears roll off her chin and drip down onto me.

"Fighter, why are you crying?"

She shakes her head, the tears falling faster now. "You're a bastard."

I frown. "I mean, I am, but I thought you would at least appreciate the 'me saving your life' part." I try to smile, try to make her stop crying.

"Not for that, although you should have told me the truth."

"That my dead wife that I suspected you of killing was, in fact, alive, although I couldn't figure out why you didn't just tell me or why my wife was on the run, and I couldn't make sense of my feelings or yours? Which part should I have told you?"

She hiccups. "I'm mad at you for not spilling your guts the second you showed up tonight. For letting me—" she gulps. "Letting me fuck four guys in front of you. That had to have been torture for you."

I grin. "It was torture, but mostly because I wanted to join them. It didn't hurt me that you were doing that. We've made no commitment toward each other—no vows, no promises. And in this world, I'm not sure we will ever be able to make promises, but that doesn't stop us from having feelings."

"I still don't understand why you let me fuck them."

"Technically, you didn't fuck them. They pleasured you, and I knew you needed it. You needed to get your anger out. You needed to heal your broken heart. You needed to know that you were strong enough without me or any other man. That way, if I'm lucky enough to have you choose me someday, it will be because you want me, not because you need me."

She touches my face, her hand caressing my cheek. I close my eyes and lean into the soft touch.

"I wasn't sure if you were ever going to touch me like this again," I whisper.

"I wasn't sure either."

Then she grabs my chin roughly to force our visions to meet, her eyes like fire. "Don't ever hide shit from me again. And don't ever push me to fuck other guys so I can get over you. I love you, you bastard. But I'm going to be pissed at you for a long, long time."

I grin like the fool I am—a fool completely and entirely in love with this woman.

"I love you too, my fighter." We still have a lot of truth left to tell each other, so much history that needs to be shared and blood that needs to be spilled. A wife and Retribution Kings need dealing with. A game is still lingering, and we need to figure out how to win or escape to be together.

All that matters right now is this moment. We love each other. When I kiss her, that's the only thought on my mind.

12

RI

I LOVE YOU—THOSE words ring in my head over and over. Lucy has said she loved me a few times, but I don't recall Vincent ever saying those words to me—or any other man for that matter.

I never knew how good it could feel.

"Say it again," I beg.

"I love you, Ri." He kisses the corner of my mouth.

"I love you, Princess." He kisses down my neck.

"I love you, Fighter." He kisses open my robe.

I gasp, my head falling back as he pushes the robe open.

"Your turn," he says, licking his tongue over the top swell of my breast.

"I hate you, Beckett," I say as his tongue halts to a stop.

"I hate you for letting another man touch me when you knew I was yours." I kiss the corner of his mouth.

"I hate you, Bastard, for letting me take my heart back when I gave it to you freely." I kiss down his neck.

"I hate you, Hero, for being willing to kill yourself in order to save me." I kiss over his heart.

91

I can hear his heart thumping slowly in his chest; each painful beat is only for me.

I kiss him hard on the lips. "I love you, Beckett, even when I shouldn't. Even when you're a married man and I'm nothing more than a prize in a game I can't win myself. I can't promise you anything. I can't promise you marriage, kids, or a life in the suburbs any more than you can promise me those things. But I can promise that no matter what happens, I'll always love you. You have my heart, and I'll protect the piece of yours that's mine with my life."

He captures my lips with his, and I melt against him. I forget everything I was thinking. I forget about how much it will hurt when I eventually lose him, either when one of us dies, when he has to return to Odette just to stay alive, or when I have to marry another man to keep him alive. Our future is going to be riddled with heartbreak and pain no matter how much we love each other.

But when he kisses me, I forget about all the pain my future holds, and I just feel him—the wetness of his tongue, the expert way he moves through my mouth, the moans he pulls from me, and the growls he makes in return.

"I'm not going to give you up. Not ever. Not for any reason. I don't know how we are going to win the game, but if I were to bet, I'd bet on us," Beckett says. "Love always wins."

I smile even though I don't believe his words.

"Kiss me," I whisper.

"I'm going to do a lot more than kiss you. You thought what the guys did to you earlier was erotic; just wait until I get through with you. You won't even consider what they did to be an orgasm," he growls.

I grin wider. There's my jealous man.

Then he lifts me up and spins me around until my ass is on the kitchen table. His eyes roam up and down my body, only covered with my robe.

"I like this—easy access," he says, flicking open the tie that's holding my robe together.

I shrug my shoulders, and the robe falls to my waist. His eyes heat at the sight of my naked body, and he bites his bottom lip, just staring at me.

I'm pretty sure I could come from that look alone. It's so fucking hot, making wetness spill between my legs.

"You're going to kill me if you don't fuck me soon," I moan.

"Then I guess we are both going to die tonight. I need to take my time with you. I need to show every part of your body how much I love it until you believe me."

"I do believe you."

He shakes his head. "You do, but it's tentative. You still think Odette is going to walk into the house, and I'm going to go run to her side."

"I don't."

"A tiny part of you does, and I don't blame you. But I'm going to change that with how I make love to you."

Chills race over my body. "No one has ever made love to me."

He cocks his head with a grin as he pushes his pants down. My eyes get hung up on my favorite appendage of his straining in my direction. "I've made love to you every time I've fucked you, and this time there will be no denying it."

Then his body covers mine as he kisses me. His lips are hot against mine as our naked bodies push against each other. My breath catches in my throat, and I know

I'm losing oxygen, but I don't care. I wouldn't stop this kiss even if it meant my death.

His hand slowly works its way down my face, over my neck, along the swell of my breast, and down to the curve of my hips. Finally, his hand lands on my thigh.

"I love every part of you—every curve, every muscle, every softness, every hardness," he says.

He kisses over my throat, pulling sharp moans from me. "I love the sounds you make when I kiss you."

His mouth tenderly kisses my nipple, and then he bites down suddenly, eliciting a yelp from me and a dirty look in my eyes.

He grins playfully. "I love your feistiness."

His hand dips between my legs, feeling the wetness there. "But most of all, I love how you make me a better man. I'm not worthy of you, but I'm going to spend my life trying to become the best man I can for you."

I don't know if I should believe him. Every other time we've made promises, we end up hurting and betraying each other. Each time I've ended up hurt, but this time feels different.

When he kisses me, he's saying he won't let anything come between us ever again. I may be foolish to let him back into my heart so easily, but for a moment, we can be happy again.

"Beckett, I need...," I moan as the ache between my legs grows. I need him inside me. I need him a dozen different ways. I need him to erase every other man's touch. I need...exactly what he's fucking doing.

His fingers push inside me, filling me as his mouth teases over my breasts. My hands run over his rippling back, pressing him hard against my body, but it's not enough.

I reach between his legs, finding his hard length. At my touch, he gasps. I almost come at the sound of his emotional cry.

We lock eyes, and we know we can't wait.

I pull him toward my entrance, and he grabs my hips as he sinks inside me one inch at a time. Every inch is like he's reclaiming my heart and soul. Each inch is a surrender of his own heart and soul. He pushes in so slowly until finally, he's sheathed himself as far inside me as he can get.

My chest rises and falls quickly against his as our fingers intertwine, mirroring our bodies.

"Is this real?" I ask as his lips lower to mine.

"As real as it gets."

Then we devour each other as his hips begin to rock. My hips angle up, meeting each of his thrusts.

He said he was making love to me every other time we've fucked, but this just feels so different. It feels like a promise of forever.

We don't say the words. We don't make the vows. We don't even voice our love to the other. We just move together, our bodies doing all the talking.

Our soft moans turn louder and more carnal.

Our movements quicken uncontrollably.

Our kisses become hungry, devouring, and painful, drawing as much blood as saliva.

We're going to wake the whole house, but maybe that's the point. Beckett looks deeply into my eyes like he's opening up his soul to me. Making sure the others hear is clearly the last thing on his mind.

My mouth parts and the sounds that escape my body are unlike anything I've heard. The softest whimpers, the loudest cries, the most desperate pleas of this happiness to never end fill the kitchen.

"I don't want this to end, Fighter, but I can't hold back much longer. I'm about to fucking explode, and I need you to go with me." The veins on his forehead fill, and I can see how much he's holding back.

I don't know how he was able to put together so many words, but I can't get anything out except a whimper.

The sound must be enough for Beckett to know that I'm close. He grins, pushing his torso harder against my clit and I come undone. I don't know the exact sound I make—a combo between a wild cat and a siren—but it explodes out of me.

I take several deep breaths, trying to come down from the high of my orgasm, when I notice Beckett on top of me, just staring at me with a shit-eating grin.

"What?" I finally pant out.

He shakes his head, smiling brighter. "You're fucking incredible."

I blush. "You are too."

He kisses me tenderly, and I feel tears welling again. Beckett notices immediately. His grin turns into a stern grimace. "Babe, what's wrong?"

I brush the tears off my face. "I'm just scared to lose this again."

He nods as I see similar tears in his own eyes. He doesn't promise we won't lose it again because he can't.

"I need you again," he whispers into my hair, still with his hard cock in me.

I feel my own need growing again as well. If I can't have him forever, then I want him as many times as possible today.

I WANT to promise her forever. I want to promise her that nothing will tear us apart, and we'll never again experience pain and loss. I want to promise her the world.

But I can't even promise her that I'll still be breathing tomorrow. The Retribution Kings may even come attack and kill me tonight. If not them, then Corsi, Ryker's men, or dozens of other groups.

She's in just as much peril. I'll do everything I can to keep her alive, but there are too many people that want to end the Corsi mafia empire. With her death, there would be no heirs, no one to inherit. The group would descend into chaos and lose all its power.

All I can promise her is now—fucking right now.

She still has doubts about my feelings toward Odette.

She is still upset about letting the others touch her when she thought the worst of me.

If I can wipe away any amount of pain or frustration, I will.

"A bed this time?" Ri asks.

I shake my head with a sly grin.

Her eyebrows raise, and she licks her lips in anticipation.

"Do you trust me?" I ask.

"I gave you my heart. Even when I pretended to take it back, it was always yours. Of course, I trust you."

I stand up, off her body still pressed against the table, pulling my cock from her. I pause for a second, enjoying the view of her spread naked in front of me—our sweat and fluids glimmer off her smooth skin.

She blushes when I slowly peruse her body. It's adorable.

I hold out my hand to her.

She takes it with a playful glint in her eyes.

As soon as she's up, I spin her back flush against my front.

She groans as I stroke down her back.

Then I kick her legs wide and press her front against the table. I grab my phone from my pants on the floor.

She yelps in surprise just like I knew she would as I press my cock between her spread legs and thrust inside her in one stroke.

"Jesus, I love you inside me," she croaks out.

I grin as I send a one-word text and then toss my phone back on the pile of our clothes. I return my gaze to her ass, focusing all my energy on her.

Thirty seconds later, the first pair of footsteps hit the kitchen floor.

The man pauses, unsure of what to do.

I grab onto Ri's hair, fisting it in a ponytail and pulling her head up. "Look up, baby."

She does and finds Ryker standing at the entrance to the hallway. His eyes are wide as he stares from her to me, his mouth agape.

He clears his throat. "I'll just go—"

"Princess, do you want him to go?" I ask, knowing she needs to decide. She felt guilty for letting them touch her, but she shouldn't. If she needs to show them how much she's mine and not theirs, then here's her chance.

The others join us a second later before she even says a word.

Gage frowns at me, unsure I should be putting on a show.

Hayes grins and crosses his arms as he leans against a doorframe. He knows exactly what this is, and he approves.

Lennox snickers and shakes his head.

"Stay," Ri gasps.

I wasn't sure if she was going to want this or not. If I talked to her about it ahead of time, she would have said no. But just like last night, when she needed them to touch her, she needs them to see she's not theirs today.

She's not mine either, though. She's Rialta Corsi— mafia princess and fierce fighter. She doesn't need any of us, but she chooses us. And right now, she's choosing me.

I need to make this quick before she loses her nerve, so I thrust hard and fast. Between my quick strokes and the added eyes on her, she'll come quick. My girl is a bit of an exhibitionist.

I'm a little overprotective, too, though. The only way I could do this is if they could see very little of her best body parts.

I grip her hair harder, knowing she likes it. I sink between her ass cheeks further and further, fucking her so hard that the table shakes.

The guys don't move. Their eyes are locked on Ri. They're all better men than me.

Her panting picks up, and I feel her tightening around my cock. She's so fucking close, and I know exactly what I want the climax to be.

"I love you, Rialta," I cry out just as she finally releases her orgasm, and I shoot my load inside her.

I may not be able to offer her a marriage, but I can at least offer her a public declaration of my love every chance I get.

"About fucking time," Hayes says with a slow clap.

I roll my eyes as I pull out of her.

I grab her robe and drape it over her before quickly yanking my pants up.

Ri takes her time pushing off the table and wrapping the robe around her. She's completely spent.

"Breakfast? Coffee?" I ask her.

Ri walks past me, straight to the kitchen.

I frown, and the others ease closer, unsure of what's next. *Did I piss her off with my little stunt? Is something else wrong?*

She can have doubts about my love for her, but I have no doubts about her love for me.

"Ri?" I ask.

Suddenly she spins and runs toward me, a kitchen knife in her hand. I'm so shocked; I don't even defend myself. The knife comes dangerously close to my heart.

"No more pretending you know what's best for me," she says, shaking the knife against my chest.

"I won't."

"No more making plans without talking to me first."

"I promise, except in life or death situations where I don't have a chance to talk to you."

She growls.

I laugh, my hand raised in front of me.

She smiles with a shake of her head. She tosses the knife into the sink before kissing me.

I drop my arm as the guys fill the kitchen.

"I don't know whether to start planning a wedding or a funeral," Lennox says.

Ri sighs. "Neither. We can't get married, not when Beckett is technically married to someone else. And Vincent would kill me if I married without his permission. And we're both too stubborn to die."

Lennox laughs at that.

Ri hops up on the corner of the counter and grabs a banana. Her robe falls open as she peels it open, revealing her glistening curves.

All eyes go to her naked body and her mouth as she starts slowly eating her banana.

The controlling, protective alpha male in me wants to rip her off the counter, carry her upstairs, and teach her about flaunting her body in front of the others. But I know that's not going to win me any points with her.

"What?" she asks, acting completely oblivious.

I raise my eyebrow, and my eyes sink into her naked flesh.

She looks down and rolls her eyes at us. "It's nothing you all haven't seen before." And then she goes back to eating her banana without a care in the world.

I half chuckle, half curse under my breath.

Ryker makes another pot of coffee while Hayes pulls out ingredients for pancakes.

Gage opens his laptop at the kitchen table, and Lennox pretends to help Hayes, although he's useless as a cook.

I walk over to Ri, about to tell her how much I miss her body already. I want us to sneak into the backyard while

Hayes finishes up breakfast, but suddenly a large Great Dane comes barreling through the kitchen.

Hayes has a stack of pancakes going, and the beast goes straight for them.

"Loki, no!" Ri yells, but it's too late.

The beast has snatched the pile and taken off through the house.

Ri winces when all eyes look at her. "That's Loki. He's Lucy's guard dog."

Lucy walks into the kitchen at that exact moment. "Oh, is that what he's supposed to be? He's more like an untrainable snuggle bug."

Ri rolls her eyes as she pats my shoulder, telling me to move so she can hop off the counter.

"He lets you know if he likes someone or not. For example, we would have never trusted Ryker if it wasn't for Loki."

"Oh, so it was Loki who convinced you? And here I thought it was my charm," Ryker says.

Ri retrieves Loki, and then we are all crowded around the animal, giving him belly rubs. Somehow the beast gets more pieces of pancake for being a 'good boy.'

"So, who are all of you?" Lucy asks.

"You've already met Beckett and Hayes. But this is Lennox and Gage," Ri says, introducing them to her.

"And you all work for?" Lucy asks suspiciously. She doesn't trust people easily, it seems, probably a smart trait.

"Me," I say, putting my arm around Ri's shoulders.

Lucy's eyes bug out. "Oh my god!" she squeals. "Are you two?" She looks back and forth between us.

"Did you not hear the racket they were making this morning? Ri's a screamer. She woke the whole damn house up," Hayes says.

Ri shoots him a scowl, which just lights him up more.

"No, I'm a deep sleeper, and this house is huge. But really? You're together? Are you getting married, because I've always wanted to be a maid of honor and I love planning weddings and—"

"Luce," Ri cuts her off with one stern word. Then Ri looks at me with a sadness I wish I could erase.

"Oh, yea, the whole game thing," Lucy says.

"Among other things," Ri says with a pause. "We are just happy to admit our love out loud. For now, that's all we can promise each other."

I take her hand and give it a squeeze.

Lucy grabs Ri's other hand. "I want to hear all the yummy details, though. Hay-boy, bring us pancakes when they are finished."

Ri flashes Hayes an apologetic look as her friend drags her outside to discuss how good I am at fucking her.

"You better hope you are as good of a fucker as you think. It would be pretty pathetic if Ri says she enjoyed us fucking her better," Hayes says.

I growl. "If you weren't in charge of food, I'd pummel your ass."

He laughs and goes back to making pancakes.

"She's a treat," Ryker says, staring at Lucy.

"Yea, she's a pain in the ass, but she's been Ri's only friend for a long time. I don't think we're getting rid of her," I say as Loki rubs up against me, begging for ear scratches. I lazily comply.

Ryker looks at me. "I know you love her, and she loves you and all of that, but she's still my responsibility to keep safe this week."

"I'll keep her safe."

"I know you will, but it sounds like you have a bigger

army after you than she does. It might be best to stay apart until you've dealt with that."

I frown, not liking the idea, but it may be true. I look to Gage behind me, the one I trust the most, silently asking him for his thoughts. He just shrugs back at me.

"You can stay around and help protect her, but I'm not going anywhere. Together we can all keep her safe," I say.

Ryker nods.

"Are you really going to stay in the game, knowing that even if you win, she'll never want you?" I ask.

"I stay in the game to protect my men. As long as I show interest in Corsi's daughter and it looks like I still have a chance, he won't attack them. He'll think that my plan to take his empire involves the game and nothing more."

"Do you have a bigger plan?"

"If I do, I won't be sharing it with you."

I grin. "Fair enough. But you're willing to die for your cause?"

Ryker nods. "I am, just like you."

"Unfortunately, the men I have left to protect are very few. Most of the Retribution Kings want to see me dead."

"They'll come around. You're new blood and will do things differently. Plus, if Odette Monroe is alive—"

"She is," I confirm.

Ryker's eyes widen. "Princess was telling the truth. I thought she was hallucinating after a broken heart."

"Nope."

"Well, then I take it back. They'll never forgive you for throwing their princess away, only to fall in love with someone else. Relationships in this world are political. They are about the joining of gangs and organizations—

making power moves. They chose you because they wanted something from the Black Empire."

"They want me to destroy them."

"Ah," Ryker says.

"Any reason you can think of that the Retribution Kings would want to end the Black Empire? Kai and Enzo rarely start fights anymore, and they just stick to themselves."

Ryker thinks for a moment. "Not sure, but my guess is an old grudge. The Retribution Kings don't let any crime go unpunished no matter how long it's been. I suspect the only way for you to get back into their good graces is to pay the price for the crime committed against them."

"That would be with my death."

"Ouch, they aren't a forgiving bunch."

Lennox glares at Ryker.

"No offense, but it's true," Ryker says.

Lennox shrugs.

"Then I would suggest you find something they want more than killing you or your family. If you win and marry Ri, you get the Corsi mafia empire. That's far more valuable than anything your brother and sister-in-law have."

I nod. "But the only way to do that is to divorce Odette, for which they'll kill me. And then convince Corsi I'm worthy of it, which will be an uphill battle. Vincent doesn't think I have anything to offer."

Ryker laughs. "You're the leader of the Retribution Kings and have strong connections to the Black Empire. And you just made an alliance with me. I'd say you have plenty to offer."

"I need to make a phone call," I say, offering no other explanation as I walk out of the kitchen. I roam through the hallways until I find a private room to make my phone call.

I have my brother's number memorized. You don't leave important numbers lying around in your contacts. And you never know when you are going to need to call for help and only have access to someone else's phone.

I dial and wait and wait and wait.

It goes to voicemail.

Strange, but not completely out of the norm.

I try Kai's number.

Siren's.

Zeke's.

Liesel's.

Langston's.

No one picks up.

I send a text to Enzo saying it's urgent.

Nothing.

I frown.

Are they in the middle of a war? Is that why no one is answering? They are all locked up in a battle and can't be bothered to answer a text or call?

I run back through the house to find Gage.

"I need eyes on my brother, on his family," I say.

Gage just nods and goes to work on his computer.

I run my hand through my hair as I pace around the kitchen. My brother and his family are in trouble, and I've done nothing to help. In fact, I've made things worse by trying to stay away from my destiny. I should be there supporting them, not here, pretending I can be a leader, pretending that I'm enough to be Ri's partner.

I'm not.

I'm not a good guy.

I've fucked up more times than I can count. I've hurt

my family. I've made poor judgments. And they will think Ri is just another mistake.

Ri makes eye contact with me from where she sits outside, listening to Lucy ramble. Ri nods her head every once in a while and smiles at her friend, but her eyes never leave mine. They notice the way my shoulders tense. They notice the veins struggling in my forehead. They notice my pacing.

Ri says something to Lucy, and then Ri is walking toward me. I stop moving, waiting for her to get to me. Only when her arms are wrapped around my body, do I breathe again.

"What's wrong?" she asks.

"I think my brother and his family are in trouble."

"Then we have to go help them," she doesn't hesitate.

I nod, my head resting on top of hers. I have my own problems, so does she. But it means the world to me that she'd drop everything to help my family.

Gage scowls at his screen.

"What is it?" I ask, still holding Ri tightly in my arm.

"They're fine, currently on Langston's private island."

"What do you mean they're fine? Are you sure they aren't being held captive? Are any of them missing?" I run over to stand behind the computer screen.

Gage tapped into their security system. He won't be able to stay long until Langston or the system kicks him out. I'm surprised he got anything.

But there they are—my entire family. They're sitting outside, around a fire pit. The adults are all drinking wine. The kids are mostly asleep in their parents' arms.

I do a quick count. Everyone is accounted for and safe. They don't look distressed.

And then Enzo looks right at the camera like he knows

I'm watching. Like they let me get a glimpse in order to prove a point.

A second later, the feed dies.

I slump back.

Ri catches me.

She's the only thing keeping me on my feet.

They all knew I was calling, and they didn't answer.

Was Odette telling the truth? Did they hurt her? Take her?

I swallow hard against the lump in my throat, but it stays lodged.

I'm suffocating; I can't breathe.

Voices are saying words to me, but I can't register them.

I fucked up in the past. My mistake almost cost the family everything, but they said they forgave me. They said there was nothing to forgive. But I couldn't stay. I found Odette. I found a way out. But...

I blink rapidly.

What if they didn't forgive me?

I'm only Enzo's half-brother. We've only known about each other for a few years. Maybe what I did was unforgivable.

A slap stings across my cheek, and I look down at the feisty woman who inflicted the blow.

"There you are. Talk to me, Beckett. What are you thinking?" she asks, gripping my cheeks and keeping my attention firmly on her.

"I'm thinking that my brother hates me. I have no family," I say, completely defeated.

I look past her at the other guys watching me.

"Do you think Odette was telling the truth? Her crazy ass story didn't make a lick of sense," Lennox says.

I shrug. "Maybe. I don't know who or what to believe anymore."

Ryker licks his lips, deep in thought.

"What are you thinking?" I ask him.

His brow furrows. "It's just...once you become a leader, that becomes the most important thing. It comes before family, before spouses, even children. It definitely comes before half-brothers. It has to. That's how our world works.

"Enzo has to put his men, his empire, before you. You're the leader of the Retribution Kings now. It wouldn't shock me if he sent a letter to them declaring war. If I was him, I wouldn't take your call. I wouldn't talk to you unless it was in formal war negotiations."

"Actually, it's his wife Kai who is in charge," I mumble back.

"Then she made the decision. She didn't have a choice. You picked your side the second you took the crown. Now you're on opposite sides."

Fuck, I'm pretty sure Ryker is right.

I won't be getting any explanations or evidence to prove that Odette's story is false.

I look at Ri. We are completely fucked.

14

RI

BECKETT FOLLOWS me to my bedroom, but I doubt there will be much sleeping tonight. It's not because we're going to have crazy animalistic sex all night, but because Beckett is a mess.

Every blood vessel in his eyes is shot, his clothes are disheveled, he hasn't taken a shower, and he's barely eaten anything all day. And he's barely talked.

I assumed it was because he doesn't trust anyone, but I'm beginning to think it's because he's hiding a sin that cuts deep.

I gently close my bedroom door and lock it as Beckett continues his pacing into my bedroom. I consider my words carefully, knowing he's close to a mental breakdown.

"Tell me why you left the Black Empire," I say.

Beckett sits on the edge of the bed, burying his face in his hand. His shoulders rise and fall violently, and I'm not sure if he's crying or just trying to catch his breath. I want to hold him, but he needs his space, too. I sit next to him on the bed and gently put my hand on his shoulder, letting him know I'm here for him.

"I can't," he eventually says.

"Why not? You can trust me."

"It's not that." He stands abruptly, pacing once again while I stay seated on the edge of the bed.

I wait for him to explain more.

"It's—I—I just can't share yet. You would think differently of me, less of me. And I just—I can't." His eyes look like he's about to spill enough tears to fill Lake Michigan. The pain he carries is overwhelming. It's more than what happened to his arm, more than what I felt when he betrayed me. He hurt someone he truly loved, possibly even killed them.

My heart breaks for him. I want to take away his pain. I want to carry some of it myself, at the very least.

"There is nothing you could say that would make me think less of you."

Beckett turns and looks at me sternly, his eyes a deep-sea of brown and agony. "This would."

"Tell me; it will make you feel better."

"I don't deserve to feel better."

I frown. "That's not true. Of course, you deserve to feel better, to not carry the pain yourself."

Beckett shakes his head. "This time, I do. It wasn't like what happened with us, Ri. I didn't protect someone I should have. They died because of me. The only reason I can even be with you is because you don't need me to protect you. I never lied when I said I can't be your hero. I'm nobody's hero."

"You're my hero, and I'm yours. Whatever happened, whatever we are going to face, we face together. But we can't do that if you don't tell me."

"It's my burden to bear."

I sigh. We are going around in circles. It's clear at the moment he won't tell me what happened. We've shared a lot of truths with each other today; maybe it's not fair to ask for more so soon.

Instead of asking again, I just sit and watch Beckett pace until he eventually talks again. "My brother wouldn't hurt me, though. None of them would."

I nod, encouraging him to say more.

"Odette has lied to me so many times. I don't believe a word she says, but I saw the video."

"Just like you saw a video of me killing Odette. You can't always believe what you see."

"Yes, but that combined with how they're reacting now... I don't know what to think." Beckett sits on the edge of the bed and then falls back in despair.

I lie down next to him as I stare at him. "Maybe your family realized that Odette was bad news, saw she was still alive, and they questioned her with the intent to return her to you. Maybe they rescued her and were about to return her to you. Maybe there's an explanation that makes sense."

"Maybe, but whatever the reason is, they should have told me, or they should have answered my call to explain to me now."

I rest my hand on his chest; he's right. So much pain could be avoided if we were all just a little more open and trusting with each other.

"What do we do now?" I ask.

"We win the game. We find a way to destroy the Retribution Kings from within. And then I talk to my brother and find out the truth."

I nod. It's all we can do, but even though our future

seems bleak, it still hurts that he didn't mention us. There was no mention of us together. I don't care if we get married. I don't care if we have to be kings and queens of a criminal organization and rule together or if we run away and hide out at the end of the earth. It makes no difference to me; I just want my life to be mine. I want the choice to be mine. And I choose him—I want him in my life.

He's not mentioning it because it's a promise that neither of us can keep, not because he doesn't love me. But I need hope, to know there is a one percent chance of being together in our future. That's all I need—one percent. Just the possibility will keep me fighting.

Beckett rolls over to look at me, and I see what he can't say in his eyes. I have to remember—baby steps. We shared a lot today. We said we love each other for the first time. We shared a lot of history and pain. That's a good start; the rest will follow. That is if we live long enough to survive it.

His lips brush mine. At first, I'm hesitant—I want words, not kisses. I want truths spoken out loud; not promises only whispered with our bodies. But as his lips brush mine, I melt against him.

I can't deny myself a chance to have him. Not when life is too short. Not when there is no promise of tomorrow or even an hour from now, not in our world.

Our lips are the only thing physically connecting us as we kiss. We don't reach out to claim more. We take our time, like two teenagers kissing for the first time and not wanting to take things too far.

His tongue parts my lips and sinks into my mouth. Mine battles back in a swirl of endorphins releasing in my body. One lick, and I need more—so much fucking more that my body literally aches for this man from my lips all the way to my toes.

"Why do I want you so much that it hurts?" I ask.

"Why can't I stay away when I'm just going to end up hurting you in the end?" he says.

Neither of us gets an answer to our question.

Our lips lock, and we don't stop again.

Our hands reach out and run up and down each other's bodies.

I never changed out of my robe, so he has easy access to my body. My struggle to reach his skin is harder, but I manage to push his shirt up enough to touch the ridges of his abs and the soft tufts of hair that disappear into his pants.

What starts off as soft and loving quickly turns rough and frantic. As much as we love each other, we are also pissed the fuck off that we love each other. Our lives would be so much easier if we didn't.

I should be focused on getting my freedom back.

He should be focused on becoming the leader he was always meant to be.

Instead, we are tangled up in each other. We're destined to be the death of the other.

"I'm not going to be gentle," he growls as he yanks on my hair to access the sensitive skin behind my ear.

"I won't either." I dig my nails into his chest until I draw blood.

Our eyes turn to fire. We are too perfect of a match for each other. Too fiery. Too independent. Too stubborn to surrender to the other.

It makes for fucking good sex, but it doesn't lead to the best decisions outside of the bedroom.

I jump on top of him and ditch my robe, straddling

him and pinning his arm above his head with both of my arms. His strength far outweighs mine, even with all of my strength pushed into his one arm. He won't let me pin him for long. I need to use better techniques if I'm going to win this battle—and this is definitely a battle.

A battle for us to keep our hearts. To stay sane. To not let our love overtake everything else. It's a battle to prove we won't let our love overwhelm us.

It's a battle we will both lose.

My teeth scrape down his chest, over his scars and the Retribution Kings' tattoo on the center of his chest.

He growls deeply; I smirk.

His hips buck, and suddenly, I'm pinned beneath him. He rips his shirt off over his head.

I grin—one step closer to him getting completely naked. I'll take that as a win. I'm naked beneath him, and his hungry eyes look over every slick spot of my skin like he owns it.

"I'm no one's property."

"I didn't say you were," he replies.

"Your eyes did."

"I'm not responsible for what you make up in your head."

I knee him in the balls, wounding him enough to grab the knife tucked in the back pocket of his jeans. We haven't brought much violence to the bedroom before, but neither of us is the lovey-dovey type. We can both only handle so much lovemaking. We need it rough and controlling and feisty.

He grins, cocking his head when he sees the knife.

"You're not going to win," he smirks.

"I'm better with a knife than you are, old man. You rely too much on your gun."

"Is that true?" he chuckles.

I nod my head slowly, my eyes peering into his completely in lust.

"You make me want to fuck you and cut you at the same time. No one else drives me so crazy like you do," I say.

He moves to pin my hands again, but I slice through the air, nicking his palm.

The deepest growl I've ever heard from him vibrates through the room.

I grab his palm with my other hand and bring it to my lips, kissing the shallow wound that I know hurts like a deep paper cut. But when my tongue brushes over it, his eyes roll back in his head, and his cock pushes between my legs. It's pure ecstasy instead.

My other hand lets the knife trace down his chest, over his tattoo that says his heart and loyalty belongs to a group that has done nothing but betray him time and time again.

He gives me a warning glare.

I smile deviously and strike through the crown with the knife, defacing the tattoo in one quick sweep.

"You're mine, not theirs."

He knocks the knife out of my hand and flips me over in one swoop. My ass is in the air pressed against his front as his hand massages it.

"And you are one wild woman who needs to be punished for cutting me not once but twice."

His hand comes down on my bare ass.

I yelp at the sudden sting and am shocked by how wet I get from having my ass slapped.

"I need to be punished more. That cut on your chest was deep; it's going to leave a mark."

He complies, slapping my ass again, pulling a deep whimper from me.

I feel sticky, warm blood from his hand as he hits my ass. It hurts him as much as it hurts me, but we both welcome the pain. It means we are alive. It means that as long as we keep feeling, we get a chance—a tiny, infinitesimal chance, but it's a chance of happiness.

"You drive me fucking crazy, Princess."

"You make me want to be saved by the handsome prince, Hero."

He growls as he almost always does when I call him Hero, but I won't stop saying it. He's my hero. I didn't need someone to physically save me, just someone to love me. That's all I've ever wanted—to be loved.

I feel him rubbing his wet and swollen cock at my ass, not my vagina.

Fuck, what did I get myself into?

I cut him, egged him on, made him bleed—of course, he's going to retaliate. He's the leader of the Retribution Kings. It's their specialty.

"Why so quiet, Princess?" Beckett asks as he rubs his swollen dick against my asshole.

"How do you always seem to win our battles?" I groan when his cock rubs from my slit all the way to my ass, spreading my wetness along the length of me.

He leans forward until his breath is hot on my back. "Pretty sure we're both going to win tonight."

Next thing I know, his cock is pushing at the entrance of my ass. I'm sweating and tense as my muscles refuse to let him in. I've been fucked in the ass before, but every time it takes some convincing.

He doesn't tell me to relax. Instead, he runs his nails down my spine, and I feel my body loosening, letting him further in. I'm reminded who's behind me. A man who loves me in every way possible. A man who wants everything from me just like I want everything from him.

It's then that I let him all the way in, that I want everything from him. I want him inside me as deep as he can go. I want him. All of him.

"Jesus, you're incredible," he mumbles almost incoherently as he thrusts inside me.

I flick my hair over my shoulder and shoot him a fiery look. He better give me the best orgasm of my life if he doesn't want me to make him bleed again.

I feel his blood on my ass as he slaps me again, sending tingles radiating through my body like tiny firecrackers going off.

"Who fucked you in the ass, Princess? Lennox? Gage? Who?"

"I—I, uh, don't know." Beckett is thrusting into me so hard and fast I can barely keep up.

"Good. When you think of men fucking your ass, you think of me."

I grin. "Jealous prick."

"When it comes to you, always. Do you understand?"

His palm comes down on my ass again when he doesn't get the answer he wants from me. I almost refuse to say anything just to feel that sweet sting again vibrating through my body and making me pant even more for him.

"When I think of fucking men, all I think about is you, Hero."

"Stop calling me Hero."

"I can't. You're mine, and I'm yours."

The next thrust pushes us to a new place, one where neither of us can talk. He pumps in and out, his hand finds my clit, intensifying my pleasure until I'm shaking, barely able to keep myself on all fours on the bed.

And then we come together. It's messy and explosive. It's everything that we are.

We collapse together on the bed. We're covered in sweat, cum, and blood. Neither of us gets up to clean off. It's the mark of each other, and there is no rush to remove that.

Beckett pulls me tightly to him, and I let him, even though I'm not sure how either of us is going to be able to sleep.

"I love you, Ri," he says into my hair. They're words neither of us were able to say when we were fucking.

I grin. "I love you too, Beckett."

15

BECKETT

He came in the night, and she's gone.

I don't know how he does it. But the night is his friend. More than his friend, it helps him lull us to sleep; it hides his footsteps; it covers his tracks.

None of us wake.

None of the security cameras catch him.

But we know who was here.

Kek.

The only man Ri is truly afraid of. The man who has the keys to controlling Ri if he wants to with one phrase. Her former friend and protector turned stalker, kidnapper.

And now he has her.

I failed.

I woke up in a sweat-induced nightmare. I reached across the bed for comfort, but she was nowhere. Not in the bathroom. Not in the kitchen. Not in the backyard.

Now, it's five in the morning, and I'm standing in the kitchen with everyone, including Lucy, trying to figure out how the hell this could have happened and how we get her back.

Gage and Lennox are on their computers, going through all the security footage to see if we can find them, but the man knows how to evade cameras. And if he used the phrase to control Ri's mind, she knows how to avoid them too. They aren't going to show up on any of the footage.

Hayes is staring out the back window like she's somehow going to show up there—not really helpful.

Lucy at least made some coffee for everyone. She hands a cup to Ryker, who takes it and slings the cup against the wall across from him. Coffee and shards of ceramic go everywhere.

No one chastises him, though. It's how we all feel.

He growls loud like a wounded animal. "How did I let this happen! I shouldn't have let her sleep in her room. I should have been with her. I should have at least had shift changes where someone was always awake. Stupid, so fucking stupid! I—"

"Ryker," I stop him.

He looks at me like he wants to kill me. I know the feeling. I want to kill myself if I let anything happen to Ri.

"This isn't your fault. It's mine. I was with her. I failed to protect her."

"Yes, but Corsi will blame me, not you if anything happens to her. And my men, my family, will suffer because I failed."

I nod slowly. "We'll get her back, and she'll be safe."

"We only have three days! And we have no clue where she is."

He's right. We don't.

I look around the room as everyone's eyes are locked on me, waiting for me to say something.

I don't have a good answer.

Just like I couldn't promise Ri that I'd marry her, that I'd spend my life with her. I can't promise them that I'll get her back before it's too late. It could already be too late. But my heart—oh, my fucking breaking heart...it needs hope. We all do.

"Rialta Corsi is the strongest person any of us know. She's a fighter. She'll survive until we find her. Or she'll escape long before we get to her because Rialta Corsi doesn't need a hero; she can save her damn self," I smirk, thinking of the times she's said similar words to me.

The security footage comes up empty.

All the places Lucy can come up with that Ri might be lead to dead ends.

Loki is useless as a scent dog.

All of Ryker's and my contacts don't have a clue where Kek is or even who he is. He's like a real-life ghost. Everyone has heard the name whispered about like a fairytale, but no one has ever met the man in real life.

It's early afternoon. We've wasted almost a full day before I start to get desperate. I call Enzo, Kai, Siren, Zeke, Liesel, Langston. I call them all. I beg for their help, not for my sake, but for hers.

No one answers.

No one calls me back.

I'm dead to them.

I'm a traitor.

I storm back into the dining room, our makeshift headquarters in the search for Ri. Everyone is out of leads. It's hard to find much when we are basically stuck in this house. If we leave, we'll have the Retribution Kings on our ass.

The Retribution Kings.

A thought hits me hard and fast. It shocks my heart that I would even consider it—a choice that will end in unending heartbreak for me. But it could save Ri, and right now, that's all I care about.

I walk over to Lennox.

"I need you to contact Caius for me," I say.

Lennox frowns from his seat behind his computer. "Are you sure?"

He doesn't ask why.

I nod. "Call him. Let me know when you have him."

All eyes are on me once again, but no one speaks. No one asks for more info on my plan. We all just want to protect Ri. Not even Ryker asks what I'm up to.

I stare down at the fresh wound Ri caused on my palm. It hasn't scabbed over yet, probably because I keep picking at it with my teeth.

"You should really let that heal," Lucy says, staring at my hand.

"I can't."

"You'll be no use to her if you have an injured hand. Follow me," Lucy says as she walks into the closest bathroom.

She opens the cabinets and quickly pulls out some ointment and bandages. She demands my hand. It's the first time I can see why she and Ri get along so well. She's just as bossy and strong as Ri but in her own way.

"You really love her, don't you?" Lucy asks as she cleans my wound.

"I do."

"I'm sorry." Lucy doesn't meet my gaze as she puts ointment on the thin wound.

"Sorry for what?"

She shakes her head. "I don't know why I said that."

"You're sorry that Ri is gone, and I'm hurting?" I lift her chin, forcing her to look at me, but I don't think that's it at all. There's something she's not telling me.

"Is there something you know, Lucy? Do you know what happened to Ri?"

"No, I don't."

"What aren't you saying?"

Lucy exhales, and her blonde hair flies. "I've always wanted her to find love, to find someone she could share her shitty life with outside of me. We are great friends, but she deserves to experience all that life has to offer. But now, I realize it was a mistake. It's just going to lead to terrible heartbreak for both of you. No matter how much you want each other, no matter how much you love each other, it will never be enough. You can't be together, not in the end."

I frown. "If one of us wins the game, then we will. If I win, I can be with her. If she wins, she can choose me. The odds are actually in our favor."

Her lips thin. "I wish it were that simple."

I'm about to question her more when Lennox pokes his head in. "I have Caius."

Lennox pushes his phone into my hand, and Lucy skirts out of the bathroom before I have a chance to question her further.

"What do you want?" Caius asks.

"I want a meeting. You, me, and Odette."

"I can't do that. I don't trust that you won't tie us up

again or try to kill us. And the others won't let us out of their sight. We can't just leave."

"Figure it out because I have a deal that will make it worth your while. Odette especially will want to hear the deal I'm offering."

I'm not sure if Caius will take the bait, but it's my only option.

"Where?" he finally asks.

"I'll text you the address. Be ready to meet in an hour." Then I hang up the phone before Caius can make any demands.

"What are we doing, boss?" Lennox asks, a little weary.

"We are getting Ri back."

———

We spent the next hour finding the perfect location and getting everyone ready. Lucy and Loki are staying at the house by themselves. Hopefully, it's safe enough, but I can't leave any men behind to watch her. Honestly, she was happy to see us go. She seemed to want to be alone.

I never got a chance to ask her any further questions, but I'm not sure if Lucy knows what she's talking about anyway.

We load up with every weapon we have before climbing into two cars to head to the restaurant. We considered an emptier building but figured Caius and Odette would better behave in a more public space. We're still prepared for an all-out war the second we leave the premises, though. I hope it's just Caius and Odette alone, but I suspect they will have brought backup just like I did.

We get to the restaurant. "I'll stay with you," Lennox says.

"No, I told them just the three of us, and that's what it needs to be—just the three of us. Gage said he can tap into the security cameras at the restaurant."

"The images aren't the best, though, so if you need us, you have to alert us. It will be hard for us to see exactly what's going on via the cameras," Gage says.

I nod.

"Are you sure you don't want a mic?" Hayes asks.

"Yes." I don't want anyone to hear the details we are about to discuss. It's too important.

No one—not Lennox, Gage, or Hayes—likes the plan. They say I'm setting myself up to be captured. I probably am, but I'll only cooperate if I get what I want first.

Ryker is the only one who doesn't seem upset with my plan. He doesn't care about my safety at the end of the day. His only goal is to find the best plan to get Ri back. And since this is currently the only plan, he's going with it.

"I'll make sure these assholes stay out here so you can get whatever info you need," Ryker says.

I nod.

"If this doesn't work, follow Ryker's lead. If he says it's worth fighting to try and get me back, then do that. But if he doesn't think you have a good shot at rescuing me, then leave me and save yourself. I need you all safe to go after Ri," I say.

"But—" they all say at once.

"Ryker is the only objective person in this car. If I'm captured or killed, you follow his lead. For the next two and half days at least, you are all on the same side with the same mission—rescue Ri at all costs. If I have to be sacrificed, so be it."

"You'll get whatever information you need, boss," Lennox says.

"Ryker is your leader until I come back. Everyone agree?"

I wait for them to all nod their heads in agreement.

"Good."

I climb out of the car and head inside the restaurant without telling them the most important part of my plan. Whether my negotiations are successful or not, I don't expect to come back.

The restaurant is swanky. I'm dressed in a suit. It's uncomfortable but surprisingly easy to hide all my weapons, so I'm not complaining.

My entire focus is on my plan to save Ri. I'm hoping for a miracle, a chance that Ri will somehow appear completely unscathed in the next five minutes, and I won't have to do this. But that's not my life. I don't get that lucky. In fact, I get unlucky. It won't shock me if Ri is found safe and sound five minutes after I do this.

Every minute that passes is a minute she might not survive. Another minute passing that I could lose her forever, so I can't waste another single minute.

"Reservation should be under Monroe," I say to the hostess.

She smiles brightly at me like I'm her favorite person she's ever seen. "Right this way, Mr. Monroe."

I vomit in my mouth when she calls me Monroe. Technically, that's the name that I said I'd go by as leader of the Retribution Kings. At the time, I wanted a connection to Odette, but now I can't run far enough away from it.

The hostess leads me to a small hidden table on the second floor. It's private, which is what I wanted, and it appears that Odette and Caius haven't arrived yet.

I take a seat and order a bottle of Odette's favorite wine while I wait. I'm not sure if they'll come, and if they do, I suspect it will be with a dozen Retribution Kings set on killing me. None of that scares me, though. What does scare me is a life without Ri.

Every time I think I've gotten Ri back, someone else takes her or puts an obstacle in our path. Every. Fucking. Time.

I drink my glass of wine without Caius or Odette showing up.

Fuck.

I realize they aren't coming after sitting for almost forty-five minutes.

I throw some cash on the table and am about to stand up when I hear her voice. "So sorry we're late, darling! My sandal strap snapped, and we had to stop by a store to pick up some new shoes."

Odette whisks over to me and kisses me on the corner of my mouth like we are a happily married couple, not a couple on the brink of war.

I let her kiss me. I don't flinch as her lips touch my skin, burning me like a hot coal. Caius pulls out a chair for her opposite me, which she graciously thanks him for before sitting. He sits in the chair next to us both a moment later.

I loosen my jaw as I look at the woman sitting across from me. The sight of her is such a stark difference from the kindergarten teacher I once thought she was. She's wearing a skin-tight red dress with her boobs popping out of the top. I'm not sure how she can breathe with how it seems to be constricting her ribs. Her hair is curled in big Hollywood waves, and she has red painted lips. Odette always liked dressing up, but I've never seen her get dolled up to this extent, except at our own wedding.

I glance at Caius out of the corner of my eye. He's in a

tailored suit with his hair gelled back. They look like they planned on attending a grand gala, not just dinner with me.

They want me to feel small like I'm out of my league. This is their world. They are used to dressing up, to playing the part. I'm not.

It doesn't matter. I didn't come here to determine who was better at playing dress-up.

"Nice of you to show up forty-five minutes late," I say.

Odette reaches across the table and brushes my hand spinning my glass of wine.

"I told you, babe, my straps snapped."

"You couldn't just wear a different pair you owned?"

She licks her lips at me as she smiles. "I needed black; silver just wouldn't do with this stress."

I roll my eyes in my head, but outside I'm stone. I don't show her any affection, but I also don't dismiss her—not until I get what I need from her.

Our waiter returns and pours Caius and Odette wine from the bottle I ordered.

"Oh, you got my favorite wine! How you know me so well, hubby."

I wince just the tiniest bit when she calls me 'hubby.' She doesn't seem to notice, but I'm sure Caius did.

"Are you ready to order?" the waiter asks.

After we all order, it's time to get to business. I've stalled long enough.

"So why are we here?" Caius asks, not happy to just have a pleasant dinner like Odette apparently is.

"First, I need to know you have no listening devices on either of you. This conversation needs to be completely private," I say.

Caius nods, assuming I would want to check. Odette just laughs. "Of course, this is a private conversation."

"Then you won't mind that I check." I pull out a small device and scan them both. To my surprise, they're clear.

"We didn't bring any men either in case you were wondering, although we did see a car of your men outside. But I do have a gun, and I have no problem using it if I need to," Caius barks.

I don't blame him for being upset with me. I took his three most loyal men and turned their loyalties to me. He would be the leader of the Retribution Kings if it wasn't for them wanting to take down my brother for some reason. My life would have been far simpler if it had turned out that way too.

"I have a proposition for you, one I think you'll both be happy with."

Caius frowns.

Odette bats her eyelashes at me.

My heart beats fast in my chest, begging me not to say the next words. It's a mistake, but this is the only way. This is the only thing I can offer that will be enough for them. This is the only way to guarantee that Ri comes back unharmed.

"I need your help getting Ri back safely."

Caius snickers.

Odette looks annoyed as hell.

"And why would we do that?" Caius asks.

"Because..." I stumble over my own words. Reluctantly, I finally force them out in a whoosh of breath and hope to god I'm doing the right thing.

16

RI

BACK AND FORTH, I rock like a baby in a cradle. I drift left then right. For a few minutes, it's rhythmic, but then it shifts just slightly, and I realize where I am. I'm on a boat. That's what the rocking is.

How did I get on a boat?

What happened?

I furrow my brow, trying to think of the last thing I remember. Beckett had a gun aimed at my head. My heart broke. I was pissed at him.

My head pounds, and my lips are dry and cracked.

How long have I been out of it? Long enough to be severely dehydrated.

I sit up slowly, afraid the light-headedness is going to cause me to pass out again.

I'm below deck in a small room, only big enough for a twin bed and a nightstand. There are no clues of who took me.

I put my hand over my chest. It hurts. It fucking aches like something I've never felt before. The loss of him, of the man I love, rips through me, breaking me in half.

I want to sob and scream and lose my mind.

But I don't feel safe here—wherever here is.

I pat my clothes for a weapon, but I find none. I open the nightstand drawer, but all I find is an old condom wrapper and a pen. Gross.

I close it quickly.

I need to leave. I need to find a weapon, something to defend myself against whoever is on this boat.

Carefully, I stand. My legs are shaky from lack of water and food. That may need to be my first mission—food, water, then a weapon. I need to find a kitchen. I can find all of those things there.

I stumble to the bedroom door and pull it open an inch to peek through the crack. There is no one in the hallway outside my door. Whoever has me has shitty security too.

I move quickly into the hallway, up the stairs, and find a small galley. There's a small fridge containing a box of pizza. I grab a slice and shovel the cold food into my mouth. Falling into the sink, I throw my mouth under the faucet for water—too exhausted to find a glass first.

After I finish a slice of pizza and have had a few gulps of water, I'm feeling well enough to search for a weapon. I open drawer after drawer, looking for a steak knife or chef's knife. I find neither, not even a butter knife.

"You were always deadlier with a knife than a gun. I couldn't take any chances."

His voice sends all the hairs on my arms into a standing position. The last man I want to be captured by has kidnapped me. I've been running from this man for years, and somehow I failed.

He must have taken advantage of my broken heart.

"You never did want a fair fight," I say, slowly turning

to face Kek.

He grins at me. His jet-black hair is cut short on the sides and longer on top; his eyes are just as black as his hair. Pits form in my stomach when he looks at me.

The rest of him is just as fit as the last time I saw him too. Muscles protrude from beneath his fitted black T-shirt and beneath his jeans.

"I don't have a knife either, so it seems fair enough to me."

"Not really when you haven't fed me or given me anything to drink in days."

He shrugs. "It's only been one day, not days. And you seem to have found enough food and water to replenish you for now. Besides, I don't want to fight with you."

I raise an eyebrow and stay alert as he walks further into the galley. I'm standing next to the island in the center of the room, keeping it between him and me as he gets closer. It won't do much to protect me, but it makes me feel better to have a chance to get away if he attacks.

"You're always looking for a fight."

"That was the old Kek; the new Kek just wants to talk."

"You kidnapped me so we could talk? You could have just sent me a text or left a voicemail; that would have been easier."

"This conversation needed to happen in person."

"So you kidnapped me and brought me to the middle of nowhere so no one will be able to find me. You do know Vincent, not to mention countless others, will be looking for me."

At least, I hope that's true. I think back to my last memory of Beckett. He wanted to kill me. He might not care about saving me. How did I escape? How did I not end up dead? Kek didn't save me, but who did?

I can't make sense of my fuzzy memories, so I suspect someone fucked with my head. I'm guessing the culprit is the man standing in front of me.

"I know, which is why we don't have a lot of time. Someone will come for you soon enough," he says.

"Vincent?"

Kek laughs. "No, but someone will."

"Are you afraid you'll lose?"

"No. I don't plan on fighting."

I frown. "So you're going to finally kill me?" I take a step back, away from him, trying to plan my escape.

Kek chuckles louder. "I'll never kill you, Princess. What fun would that be?"

"You really brought me here to talk?"

He nods.

I suck in a breath. "What do you want to talk about?"

I'm on high alert. I don't trust Kek; I never will. He killed someone I loved. I've barely survived his past games, and I can't imagine what game he's playing now.

He opens his mouth, and I know the phrase he's about to say.

Fuck.

I cover my ears and start screaming at the top of my lungs. I refuse to let him control me anymore. I run out the galley and up the stairs to the top deck of the boat, not really sure what I'm going to do next. But I'll jump in the water and start swimming if it comes to it.

I'm hoping to find a weapon, anything I can use to kill him once and for all. Or something to kill myself with because I'd rather die than let him torture me again.

Kek is right behind me. I keep screaming and yelling, trying to block out any words when I hear the rumble of an engine. Someone is nearby.

I change my screams to cries for help. I don't know who the nearby boat belongs to, and I may be signing their death sentence if the boater isn't from this world and prepared to fight, but I have to try. It's my only hope.

I wave my hands frantically in the air as the boat nears, and I see blonde locks sticking out from under a man's ball cap.

I let out a sigh. It's not entirely who I was hoping for, but he'll do.

Kek grabs my arms and whips me around to face him. I'm still yelling, still trying to block out his words—just a few seconds longer, and I'll have help. Kek is a good fighter, but his best strength is being able to control me. He already said he doesn't plan on fighting. I have to hope he was telling the truth.

Kek's eyes are wild and desperate. There's a flicker of fear in them.

I've never seen him like this. I don't understand it.

"Stop, just listen. I won't use the phrase. I just need you to hear me."

"I don't trust you."

"I know, and you shouldn't."

The boat lurches—Caius's boat must have hit ours. We have seconds, not minutes, until he'll be here.

Footsteps make their way onto the top deck, and I know Kek is about to make his grand disappearance.

"Don't trust them, any of them." Kek pushes me away toward Caius when he says one last phrase that doesn't make sense to me. "Give him up."

And then Kek is gone.

I frown. *That was what was so important? For Kek to tell me not to trust anyone?* I already knew that. There had to be something else I'm missing.

Caius runs to me and pulls me into his arms. I let him. It feels good to be held again.

"Are you hurt?" Caius asks.

"No."

"We need to go after him." He pushes a gun into my hand.

I take it, but it's no use; Kek is gone. It's one of his greatest abilities—to be able to disappear without a word. He can just be gone like a shadow in the night.

Caius won't believe me, though, and I want to see with my own eyes that Kek is gone.

"Stay close to me. I don't want to let you out of my sight," Caius says.

I want to argue that I can defend myself, but when it comes to Kek, I don't feel comfortable being by myself. So I follow Caius as we check the top deck and then the rooms below.

"I don't understand; he's just gone," Caius says.

I nod. "I never understood it either, but he's very good at disappearing when he wants to."

I look at the boat Caius brought. "Anyone else come with you?"

He shakes his head. "Just me. We all followed separate leads. The Retribution Kings are doing everything they can to try and find you."

He doesn't mention Beckett.

"Even when they almost had me killed before?"

"They realized their mistake." Caius looks at me with longing eyes as he searches mine for something. He's probably looking for any amount of affection that I might have toward him.

"Thank you for saving me," I say.

He holds out his hand toward me, and I take it. "Anytime."

He helps me onto his boat and wraps a blanket around my shoulders. I sit down in one of the two captain chairs, and we start driving toward shore. Looking around now, I realize we're on Lake Michigan.

"What do you remember?" Caius asks.

I stare out at the water. "I remember Beckett almost killing me and then nothing. I don't know how I got from that point to Kek taking me."

Caius sighs. "We helped you—Lennox, Hayes, Gage, and me. Beckett didn't tell any of us his plan, but we knew it couldn't be true. We got you out of there, and then Odette came back, so we knew we were right."

I'm holding my breath, I realize.

"And Beckett?"

He turns his head to look at me slowly out of the corner of his eye as he holds the helm. "He only has eyes for Odette. They've been inseparable since he got back. I think he realizes his mistake when it comes to you, and he's sorry, but all he cared about was being with her.

"Odette's the love of his life. He thought he lost her. It broke him in a way we didn't think was repairable. He used you as a distraction and to help get her back. But now that she's back, he's consumed with her and making sure that no harm comes to her."

My throat closes up, and my heart seizes. I'm not even sure if it's pumping blood anymore; it doesn't really see the point.

I close my eyes, trying to remember, but I can't find anything in my memories that could contradict Caius's words.

"I'm so sorry," he says, slowing the boat down until he

can walk over and wrap his arms around me.

It's then that I release the tears—full out sobs into his shoulder. I can't hold them back any longer.

I'm embarrassed with how long I cry, but it's nice to have Caius holding me in his arms. It's nice to feel loved even if I don't love him back.

"I'm sorry," I say, rubbing the tears and snot on the corner of the blanket.

He chuckles. "Don't be. I care about you, Princess. I'm here for you whenever you need a friend or more."

There's so much hope left in his voice when he says 'more.' I don't want to squash the hope of my savior, but I'm not sure anything can change my feelings for Caius. He's a nice guy, but not someone I could love. Maybe that's what I need, though. A man who's strong and kind, but not a man I could fall in love with. A man who can't hurt me. A man who could be a partner, not a lover.

There aren't many men left in the game. If I had to choose one of them, Caius wouldn't be a bad choice. I wouldn't be surprised if Beckett bowed out of the game now that Odette's back.

It's between Caius, Ryker, and three others.

Caius might be my best choice.

I lean into his shoulder, now damp with my tears.

"What would I do without you?" I ask.

He pushes my hair back and then kisses my forehead. "I don't know what I would do without you either."

It feels right and wrong at the same time to be in his arms, but I need the strength right now. I need the support, so I take it.

Then Caius whispers something into my ear that I can barely make out. If I wasn't sure where Caius's loyalties lie, I am now.

BECKETT

Waiting sucks.

I have no idea if my plan is working. No idea if Ri is safe. No idea if the sacrifice I made is worth it. And I don't know how long it's going to take for her to be safe.

I can't breathe until I know Ri's safe. I did something crazy and ruthless to get her back. And if it doesn't work, I still have to keep my end of the deal. I'm trapped, and it would all be for nothing if she wasn't safe.

"Honey, you've hardly touched your food," Odette says from my left. We're sitting at the center of a long table, looking out at the Retribution Kings celebrating our union.

The crowd is jubilant. They drink and eat and laugh like this is a true celebration. I'm the only one who knows the truth.

Hayes, Gage, Lennox, and Ryker sit to my right at the long table as my closest men. All of them stare at me like I've lost my fucking mind.

Hayes keeps shaking his head at me in disappointment.

Gage shoots daggers in my direction.

Lennox can't stand to look at me, and anytime anyone makes a toast, he laughs instead of cheers.

Ryker is the only one who keeps his emotions to himself. He either doesn't care about me as much as the others, or he knows—he knows the only reason I'm sitting here acting like Odette is my queen is because I did something to get Ri back.

It's better that they don't suspect, though. It's better that I'm the only one who knows. I'm going to have to keep this up for days, weeks, years—locking my secret away in my own mind will help keep me up the charade.

My heart is Ri's, not Odette's, but I can never show that truth. It's the only way to keep Ri safe from Kek, from the Retribution Kings.

Odette leans into me. I do everything not to stiffen. I smile lovingly back at her because I know what she wants, and I'm forced to give it to her.

I've given Odette everything of me—my body to do what she pleases with, my kingdom I fought so hard to win, my power, my very soul—it's hers.

But I kept my heart. It's locked away for Ri, for the hope that someday it could be hers in a real way. But that's a lost hope.

I lean into Odette and kiss her for the hundredth time tonight. She's insatiable, and every second I'm kissing her is pure torture. I'd rather be stabbed repeatedly in the chest than kiss her, but this is the sacrifice I made, and soon, I should know if it was worth it or not.

I pull my phone out, waiting for a text or call from Caius to let me know she's okay. But there's nothing.

I put the phone on the table next to me so I can see the second he sends a message. Odette gave Caius the info he needed to find Ri. She knew more about Kek than even I suspected. She knew the phrase to help unlock Ri's mind. She knew how to find Kek. It only makes me more suspicious of Odette, but I don't give a shit what lies Odette has told me if it saves Ri.

If I'm to live this life, I need to know that Ri is alive and her mind is her own. Ideally, I need her free of the dangers, free to chose her own husband, free to be her own woman. But that might be too much to hope for her. Alive and her mind uncontrolled might be the best I can do for her.

Caius may not be my greatest ally, but he cares about Ri. He'll do everything he can to find her.

At least, that's what I keep telling myself. Caius will find her. He'll call. He wants Ri safe, and he wants his sister happy. He'll do the right thing.

The back door of the banquet hall opens. I barely pay attention to it; people have shown up late all night through that door. But this time, raven-colored hair catches my attention.

My heart stops when I see them. Caius has his arm and a blanket around Ri's shoulders. She looks exhausted. I can tell her eyes are red and swollen from here. She leans her head into his chest like a lover. Despite her eyes, she has a soft smile on her lips.

Caius looks concerned as if now that he's brought her back, I won't keep to my promise. But I know what will happen if I don't.

Odette says something that the others at the table laugh at, so I join in. It's a deep, belly laugh, the kind that Odette used to swoon at. Swoon she does when she hears it again.

"It's so good to hear you laugh again," Odette says, resting her hand against my chest.

"It feels good to laugh again now that you're back in my life." I grip her hand, pretending it's Ri's, and then I kiss her.

I don't look at Ri. I don't watch for her reaction. I'm not sure if Ri will believe my act, but I'd rather break her heart now than slowly over days. It was never going to be me. I was never going to be enough.

Ri calls me a hero. I guess I am, and she'll never know it. I saved her from the worst, but now she's going to have to find a way to save herself from the rest.

When I break from Odette's lips, I put my classic shit-eating grin, complete with dimples, on my face and laugh like this is the greatest day of my life.

Man, I'm sick. This is my life now—playing politics and pretending to care for the woman who betrayed me. All while the real woman I want is sitting in the same room.

I can feel their eyes on me, the guys next to me.

"Are you not going to go check on Ri?" Hayes, the closest to me, asks.

"Nah, she looks fine from here. Ryker should be happy that Corsi isn't going to kick his ass now that she's back safe and sound."

None of them blink as they stare at me, trying to find out what demon is inhabiting my body right now. It's me guys; I'm just saving Ri the only way I know how.

Slowly, one by one, they all get up and walk over to her.

I refuse to look in her direction. I refuse to torture myself. And I have to play the part of disinterested leader who's elated to have his wife back.

Wife—ugh. What the hell was I thinking, getting married when I barely knew her?

Ri is safe. Ri is with the men who care about her the most. They'll help her get through this, probably fuck her again like last time—the bastards.

And then Stan walks over, ruining my fake pleasant mood.

"What do you want?"

"For you to get retribution against the Black Empire for your incredible wife," Stan says.

I frown as I wrap my arm around Odette's shoulders. "I have her back; we're happy. I'm not going to start a war."

He smirks. "I'm glad to see the happy couple back together, but you don't have a choice. If you want to stay married to Odette and, you know, breathing, then you have to get retribution. We are the Retribution Kings. We didn't get that name from just living happily ever after with our wives. We got the name from exacting revenge. Now, declare war or I'll have you killed tonight in your sleep."

He walks away and talks to someone else at the head table before I have a chance to argue back.

"Can't you tell everyone you made a mistake? My brother and his family had nothing to do with your disappearance," I hiss to Odette.

She bats her long eyelashes in my direction. "And why would I do that when it's not true?"

"I'm giving you everything you want. I'm being the doting husband. I'm leading the Retribution Kings. Isn't it enough?"

Her eyes drag up and down my face before she says, "No, it's not enough."

I blink, not believing I'm hearing the coldness in her

tone. I thought she was the sweet, kind woman I fell for. I thought she genuinely cared about other people. I couldn't be more wrong.

"If you love me, you'll do this for me," I say.

"I would if you really loved me, but you still love her. I'm glad you made the right decision to be with me, but I won't be made a fool of. You're not as good an actor as you think. I can see through you easily enough, so I'm sure others can too. Now, declare war, or you won't be the only one dying in your sleep." Odette's eyes slither to Ri, and I realize just how trapped I am. I'm going to have to declare war with my brother to save the woman I love.

Forgive me, brother.

18

RI

BARELY ANYONE PAYS us attention when we walk into the banquet hall. It's strange not to be the center of attention, but I like it.

The only people who do see us are the table at the far end of the room. Everyone is staring in their direction, which is why they don't notice Caius and me.

Beckett, Odette, and the guys notice me.

Beckett pretends he doesn't.

Odette pretends I don't phase her.

And the guys stare at me like they've seen a ghost.

Beckett laughs. It's a beautiful laugh, the kind I don't think I've ever seen.

Hmmm...

Then he pulls Odette against his lips in a big show of their love and affection for each other.

I stop walking when they kiss and study them like animals in a zoo exhibit.

Caius stumbles to a stop next to me. His arm is draped around me, shielding me as best as he can.

"You okay?" he asks, looking from me to the happy couple.

I check my feelings expecting to feel immense pain, heartbreak, or rage. Instead, I feel nothing—just nothing—no feelings whatsoever watching them.

Strange.

I nod. "I'm hungry. Let's find a table to eat."

Caius leads me to an empty table toward a quieter corner of the room. He flags a waiter down and orders for me, so I don't have to think. He probably thinks I'm in shock.

He thrusts a glass of water in front of me and tells me to drink. I comply.

Next, a plate of food is brought over. Chicken, potatoes, macaroni—comfort food.

I dig in, not caring what the food is.

I'm mid-chew when I hear footsteps approaching our table. I look up to see them all stop suddenly, staring down at me like I'm an alien.

"Are you going to join us or just stare?" I ask.

They all take a seat at once.

I look from each face to the next. All of them look solemn and frightened of me like I'm going to punch them.

"What's wrong?" I ask before shoveling more food into my mouth. I'm starving; I can't believe how hungry I am. I don't know what tomorrow is going to bring, but I need to regain my strength.

Hayes looks from me to Beckett. I let my eyes follow his gaze. "Are you okay with…"

I reach across the table and grip his hand. "I'm fine, just hungry."

"Are you really okay? Kek didn't hurt you?" Lennox asks, worry threading his voice.

I nod. "I'm fine. He locked me in a room. Maybe fucked with my memories a little, but otherwise, I'm perfectly fine. No broken bones. No scars. No bullet wounds."

They all look at me suspiciously, and I can tell the question they want to know, but none of them have the balls to ask.

"He didn't rape me," I say, putting them all out of their misery.

They all exhale at once as if they couldn't breathe until they knew.

I roll my eyes. But it's nice how much they care.

Caius rubs my back, and I don't flinch away.

Gage especially stares at the contact like he can't believe what he's seeing. Ryker is the only one who hasn't shown strong emotion.

"I need to talk to you," I say, putting my fork down.

"We're here to listen," Hayes says, with a tiny playful smile.

"Individually," I say, looking from him to the others.

Everyone nods, and Lennox, Gage, and Ryker all stand. I look to Caius. "Leave us."

He frowns but then stands. "I'll get you something to drink. What do you want?"

"Red wine."

He nods and then heads to the bar. Hayes is left at the table to speak with me alone first.

"Has Caius—" Hayes starts.

"No, Caius has been a perfect gentleman. He rescued me."

"That's why you are being so nice to him?"

I nod but don't say more. I don't know who to trust anymore.

"So why do you want to talk to all of us alone?"

"I want to know about Beckett."

Hayes frowns. "I'll tell you anything you want to know. But why do you need to hear from us separately?"

"I just think my heart will believe it more if all of you tell me on your own that Beckett is in love with Odette."

Hayes's shoulders slump. "I can't tell you who he loves. Honestly, I don't understand a thing about him anymore."

I raise my eyebrows at him, imploring him to get to the point.

He sighs, rubbing the back of this neck. "I don't know. He either loves her, or he's putting on quite an act." Hayes must read the disappointment on my face because he adds, "That doesn't mean he doesn't love you too. You could still win him back! It just—"

"It's okay, Hayes. Can you call Lennox over?"

Hayes gets up, and I let Hayes's words settle into me before Lennox sits down.

"You want to talk about Beckett?" he asks.

I nod. He could always read people better than anyone else.

He considers his words carefully. "Let him go, Princess. Whether he loves you or her makes no difference. He's made his choice."

"Thank you for your honesty."

"I'll send Gage over."

A few seconds later, Gage is sitting in front of me.

"Does Beckett love Odette?"

"Yes," Gage answers in a single word. No other explanation. No sugar coating it. No 'but he loves you too' speak.

I nod.

He doesn't say more. He just gets up and tells Ryker it's his turn with me.

Ryker is the only one who smiles at me when he sits across from me. "It's good to see you, gorgeous."

"That's only because you needed to save your own skin."

He laughs. "Partially, but also because I've become fond of you, kiddo. And I want to finish the games. I think I have a good shot at beating Charming over there." He points to Caius.

"And the dickhead on the throne." He motions to Beckett.

"I doubt the dickhead on the throne will be competing much longer. Why compete for me when he already has a wife?"

Ryker falls back in his chair. "That's what you wanted to ask us. Do we think Beckett loves her or you?"

I grit my teeth, feeling stupid asking them all the question, but I need to know what Ryker thinks, perhaps more than the rest.

He studies me for a moment as if somehow, I have the answer displayed somewhere on my body.

"I think you're asking the wrong question."

"Huh?"

"I don't think it matters who Beckett is in love with. It matters who you love. You have a lot more power and control over your destiny than you realize. If you love him, go get him."

I frown. "That easy, huh?"

"Of course."

"And I don't suppose you love anyone?"

"That is a moot point. We aren't talking about me;

we're talking about you. Stop listening to everyone. Stop paying attention to his actions. Listen to your own heart. If you want him, go get him. If you don't, let him go."

"What if I want him, but it would hurt more people to go after him than it would if I let him go?"

Ryker frowns at me. "I can't answer that for you. That's something only you can decide."

The others join us, and we all drink wine together. Hayes makes jokes. Caius rubs my back. The others alternate glares between Caius and Beckett.

That is until Beckett is handed a microphone.

He stands with Odette at his side. She holds onto his shoulder as he holds the mic with his one hand.

"Thank you all for coming here to celebrate me getting Odette back. I don't know what I'd do without her."

Beckett leans over and kisses her forehead as she beams.

I notice that no one at my table claps.

"I hope you have all enjoyed yourselves tonight, and you've gotten plenty to eat and drink."

Everyone mumbles their agreement.

"Good, because I have a serious announcement to make."

The room goes silent, and I stop breathing. *What could he announce that's worse than being married to her?* She's pregnant—that would crush me. It would mean he's been with her while he was with me. What a fool I've been.

"As you all know, Enzo Black was one of the men responsible for taking my wife from me. We are going to get retribution for those weeks of torture where I thought the love of my life was dead. We are going to war with the Black Empire."

The room breaks out in cheers. Everyone is happy

except our table, once again. My table looks at him in disgust, like they can't believe what they are hearing. Even Caius seems disturbed.

Then Beckett's eyes land on mine. They are empty and vacant. I don't know if he loves her or me, but I know he loves his brother. I know he played a part in Caius finding me.

Ryker told me it didn't matter what Beckett felt; it matters what I feel. He's right. I still love Beckett, even if I want to kill him.

My final act of love will be trying to stop this war.

19

RI

"Ready to go to bed?" Caius asks me as the ballroom slowly starts clearing.

The others glare at him.

"What? I didn't mean go to bed with me, just go to sleep," Caius snaps back.

I put my hand on Caius's arm. "I knew what you meant." I yawn, stretching my arms. "And yes, please."

I'm not sure where we are all going to sleep, but I'm more than ready to stop watching Beckett and Odette's displays of affection, real or fake.

I stand up, and Caius leads me outside, followed by the others. The sun set hours ago, and there's a chill in the air. I shiver, and Caius is right there to put the blanket I left behind in the banquet hall around me.

"Thanks," I say with a soft smile.

"Of course." He puts his hands in his pockets as we walk toward a nearby hotel where Caius has rooms reserved for the night. The others follow behind.

No one speaks about Beckett's declaration of war. No one knows what's going on in his head anymore, and no one wants to speculate. That, or they don't want to bring up his name around me in case it hurts me.

We reach the hotel, and Caius goes to the desk to collect our keys.

He returns and holds out a key for me.

"What about everyone else?" I ask.

Hayes runs up to me and puts his arm around my shoulders. "We aren't letting you out of our sight again."

"Since that worked so well the last time," Lennox grumbles.

Hayes frowns. "Well, this time, we'll do shifts, so someone is awake at all times. We won't let anyone through, not this time. We promise."

"Don't make promises you can't keep," I say.

Hayes's scowl deepens.

Caius starts walking toward the elevators, and I follow. Then we are all riding up to the top floor, where we will all be sharing a room. But when Caius opens the door, I realize it's a suite taking up half the floor. There are plenty of places for the guys to crash that aren't two feet away from my bed—thank god.

"I'm going to shower," I say, walking through the suite to the main bedroom and ensuite bathroom.

Every guy in the room starts following me.

I snap my head back toward them. "Alone."

Lennox and Hayes chuckle. "We aren't going to stand in the bathroom with you, but we need to do a quick sweep first. Then someone will be outside your door at all times," Lennox says.

I roll my eyes but let the guys pass. Every single one of them heads into the bathroom like they don't trust the others to do a security sweep.

Finally, one by one, they file back out. "All good?" I cross my arms over my chest as I smirk at them.

"All good," Gage says.

I walk into the bathroom. Apparently, Hayes got bathroom duty because every five minutes, he hollers into the bathroom, and I have to holler back to keep him from breaking down the door.

I sigh as the hot water pours over me. So much for a hot, relaxing shower in solitude to wash away the pain of the day.

I find a robe on the back of the door and wrap it around me rather than putting my dirty clothes back on. I open the door to find all five of the guys inspecting the bedroom or lounging on the bed.

"You do know this place has a lot more space than just this one room, right?" I say, toweling off my hair.

Their eyes zero in on my body, peeking out a little too much thanks to this loose-fitting robe, but I don't care. I'm not Beckett's. And I'm comfortable. I'm not ashamed of my body, but it doesn't mean I'm going to fuck any of them either.

I walk over to the edge of the bed and climb up as no one responds to my snarky comment.

"What?" I finally ask, knowing there is something they aren't telling me.

"Corsi called," Ryker says.

I frown, and all the warmth in the room leaves. "What did he want?"

"To talk to you."

I take a couple of deep breaths. I don't know if he was behind Kek kidnapping me. I don't know what crazy thing my father demands of me now, but I need to talk to him.

"Get him on the phone," I say.

Caius pulls out his phone and dials a number, then hands the phone to me.

I take it, unsure if the others should be listening to this conversation or not, but I doubt I'll convince any of them to leave. Even if I do, Gage will just fasten something to listen through the door.

"Hello," Vincent's deep voice comes through the phone.

"Vincent, you called?"

"I did. I'm surprised you returned my call so quickly. You have a tendency not to follow my directions."

"Just trying to keep you on your toes."

He ignores me. "I thought you'd like to know that you get to pick the next game."

My eyes shoot out of my head. I wasn't sure my father really considered me part of the game. I didn't think if my name was selected, he'd actually let me choose the game.

"Do I need to tell you ahead of time?" I ask.

"I'll summon you about an hour before the game is supposed to start. That should give us enough time to set up whatever you have planned."

Suddenly, the phone line goes dead.

He ended the call without a goodbye or a chance for me to ask any other questions.

I lower the phone, still in shock.

"What did he want?" Caius asks.

"I get to choose the game."

Everyone's mouth drops.

"I know," I say, my own mouth hanging open.

"Do you know what game you'll pick?" Gage asks.

I shake my head. I honestly don't.

"If you could give me a heads up, Princess, I'd appreciate it. I'd like to not die this week," Ryker says.

I smile at him. "I'll make sure it's a game that won't end in your death. Maybe just seriously injured," I tease.

He laughs.

I get to pick the game.

I could pick something that plays to my strengths. Something I could win and have all the power. If I won, would I get to take care of myself for the week instead of having to live with others?

I don't know if Vincent would ever allow that.

I climb into the bed, exhausted and tired of violence. Whatever game I choose won't be violent. It will be civilized, maybe something to help my father actually see the men's merits. See why they would or wouldn't make a good husband for me.

It probably won't help, and the next week someone else will come up with another violent game. But at least this time, I can do something that won't end in death this week.

I close my eyes as ideas start spinning in my head. The guys make themselves comfortable on the floor around me in silence.

"This bed is big enough for at least one or two more. Not everyone should sleep on the floor," I say.

There's some hushed mumbling, and then I feel two bodies climbing into the bed, one on either side of me.

I smile and peek my eyes open to see Hayes on one side and Caius on the other.

I'll sleep well tonight.

The sounds come. They're muffled at first, but they grow stronger with every bang of the bed against the wall.

I can't breathe, I'm suffocating, this is my worst nightmare.

I don't think the others realize who it is at first. They,

after all, are not intimately familiar with the sounds one of them makes like I am. But after a minute of the sound coming through the wall, there is no denying who is on the other side and what they are doing.

How could they end up in the room right next door?

My memories are fuzzy about the last couple of days. I thought I was okay with Beckett choosing Odette. As long as he's happy, I'm happy for him. But this...this breaks me—every moan, every bang of her head against the head-board, every cry of his name.

The tears fall, and they don't stop.

20

———

BECKETT

ODETTE IS in the bathroom doing god knows what. I quickly climbed into bed and am hoping to be fast asleep before she comes out. I doubt I'll ever sleep again, though. I have too many thoughts in my head—about Ri, about my brother.

I declared war tonight. If my brother wouldn't talk to me before, he won't talk to me now.

And I don't know how to put a stop to any of it.

I need to find a way to send a message to Kai and Enzo to warn them, to tell them I don't want this.

I can try to delay things as long as possible. I can convince the Retribution Kings we need to see how the game plays out with Ri and what Corsi does. We may need his army. I doubt they will let me keep playing in the game, though.

Delay—that's all I can hope to do. I've decided my fate. I've done all that I can to save Ri, *but will it be worth the cost?*

How do I protect Enzo and Kai?

I smirk. I don't.

161

They are more than capable of winning a war against these idiots. And if I help steer the Retribution Kings in the wrong direction, their odds increase. Kai won't let anything happen to her family.

My head falls back on my pillow, a bit relaxed for the first time. My family will destroy the Retribution Kings, and then I'll be free. They'll be pissed at me, more pissed than all the other stupid shit I've done combined, but I'll willfully spend my life making it up to them.

The bathroom door opens; I squeeze my eyes shut and calm my breathing. I meditate to stay as still as possible, so Odette thinks I'm asleep as she comes to bed.

She doesn't say anything, not even a whisper of my name. Maybe she's had a long day too and just wants to sleep.

I feel the bed shift and the covers move as she climbs into bed. I don't move. I don't know if I'm a snorer or not. I don't know the typical sounds I make when I sleep, but I'm hoping it's silence.

Odette rolls over to me and kisses me sweetly on the forehead. Thank god. She's just going to kiss me goodnight.

"If you want her to live through the night, you'll stop faking sleep and fuck me."

Her words are ice cold and delivered to make an impact.

I open my eyes but still don't move.

"Ri helped you. She helped you escape when you thought you had no options. Why would you kill her?"

"Because you prefer her to me. You don't belong with her; you belong with me. You don't want a girl who can hold her own on a battlefield right next to you. You want a girl who will be waiting at home with a good meal and warm bed when you return."

"You can't cook."

"I can learn."

I grunt. "Don't threaten her life. If you want something from me, then figure out how to convince me."

I roll on top of her, pinning her to the bed and tightening my hand around her throat, making it difficult for her to breathe. "Don't threaten Ri ever again, or I'll kill you. Understand?"

I scare her like the monster I am. She's destroyed my life, and I want to end her. But I can't—at least not until Ri is completely safe. Ri needs to have run away or married a man who is strong enough to protect her.

I cringe at that thought.

She nods, but when I release her throat, she becomes maniacal. Her nails dig into my skin, and she cackles like a cartoon villain.

"I own you, Beckett. You can't threaten me without threatening her. You needed Caius's help to save her. He did that, but he's also getting close to her. He might have even fucked her in her misery over losing you. He's slowly gaining her trust. And he's got the best shot of winning the game and marrying her."

If I could kill her with a look, then I would. My eyes brand my hatred into her body.

"If you don't do exactly what I say, if you so much as lay another finger on me, and most definitely if you kill me, Caius will end her. Caius likes her. He'd love for her to be his wife, but he loves me. He's loyal to me. He'd do anything to avenge his sister's death. So threaten me again and see what happens. Mark me again, and I'll let him know exactly where to put the same marks on her body."

My eyes well with tears, but I don't let them out.

"What do you want?" I ask with as much strength as I can muster.

She grins, knowing she's won. And she has, but she won't always.

I don't regret tying her life to Ri's. It means Ri is safe. Caius and the Retribution Kings will do everything to keep her safe. But someday, Odette will get what's coming to her.

"I want you to fuck me like I'm her."

I swallow hard against my throat. That's impossible. I can't fuck anyone like I do Ri. It will never be the same.

Odette undoes the robe she's wearing, revealing some red lacy lingerie. There was a time when I would have found her sexy as hell. Now I want to throw her into the depths of hell.

"Beckett, I'm waiting." Odette just lies spread out on the bed, waiting for me to do all the work.

Fuck, it would have been so much easier to just let her ride my dick. I should have let her take from me and not be an active participant.

God, how am I going to do this?

I'm just wearing my boxer briefs as I position myself over her body. Just two thin pieces of fabric separate us.

It's just sex. Just fucking, I try to convince myself.

It's just putting my heart and soul in a shredder. This will destroy me. I'll never forgive myself. Ri won't either. I won't ever be able to fuck a woman without thinking about this moment. This mistake. This...

Odette sinks her nails into my chest, drawing blood. I curse.

"Get on with it, baby. I've been waiting a long time to have you again."

My cock is anything but hard.

I remove it from my briefs and close my eyes, thinking of Ri. Of what snarky comment she might say to me. Of her red lips wrapped around my cock. Of her whimpers and cries when I touch her.

A hand reaches out and strokes my length. I squeeze my eyes shut tighter.

It's Ri. It's Ri. It's Ri.

I moan as the hand pumps me. It does feel good.

And then I'm guided toward her entrance.

I keep my eyes shut, my arm trembling against the headboard. The second I feel a drop of moisture on my cock, I thrust hard, ripping through her. I thrust viciously. If I don't, I won't be able to stomach it.

I pound as hard as I can. I'm out of breath, so is she. I hear her head hitting the headboard.

Ri.

Ri.

Ri.

I force myself to think of her, not reality.

Every part of my body knows it's not her, though. No matter how tightly I squeeze my eyes shut, I can't keep tears from dripping down my face and onto hers.

She cries out, and I know she's orgasming.

"Come with me, baby," she purrs.

I can't. There's no fucking way I can or will. But I go through the motions. I make the fake sounds, the fake grunts, and jerks into her body.

She doesn't call me out.

I open my eyes to see her smirking in victory up at me.

I pull myself out and off of her as fast as I can, heading to the bathroom before she can protest. I intend to shower to wash her stench off me, but I don't make it that far, vomiting violently into the toilet first.

I'll never forgive myself. That was too much. I made too many mistakes that led me here. I've never felt so much despair, emptiness, darkness. All I really want to do right now is find Ri and tell her to hold me as she drives a dagger into my heart to make the pain stop.

21

RI

"I WANT to take you somewhere before we leave to meet Corsi tonight," Caius says.

We've been eating breakfast in the hotel room, taking our time drinking several cups of coffee and a couple of rounds of breakfast. No one slept very well last night between Beckett and Odette fucking, half of them sleeping on the floor and waking up at various hours all night to change security shifts.

I set my third cup of coffee down on the kitchen table. "Okay."

"Where are we going?" Hayes asks.

Caius frowns. "I meant just Ri and me."

Hayes looks baffled with his unkempt hair and glasses sitting crooked on his face. "But—"

I give Hayes a look. "I'm supposed to meet Vincent in two hours. Nothing is going to happen to me between then and now."

Hayes looks to Ryker for help.

Ryker looks at me. "Wear a tracker? And don't get

kidnapped. I need to meet with some of my guys before tonight anyway."

He kisses my cheek.

"Thank you," I whisper, knowing he's ultimately the one who gets to decide. It will be his ass if anything happens to me.

I need a moment away from everyone's pity glances, anyway. I'm the foolish girl who fell in love with a man who always loved someone else.

Hayes turns to the others. "Help me out here. She shouldn't be going anywhere alone, especially not with hi—"

"I think it would be good for you to get some fresh air," Gage says to me.

"I agree. You two should talk; clear the air. We need to find Beckett and see what the hell he wants us to do anyway," Lennox says.

Hayes looks at both of them like they've lost their minds. "We're not still going to do what that idiot says, are we?"

Gage and Lennox ignore him.

Ryker brings me a simple bracelet with a small emergency button to wear as a tracker. If I take it off, it sets the alarm off as well.

After gulping down the rest of my coffee, I'm ready to go.

Caius and I walk out of the building silently. I did my best not to look at Beckett and Odette's door as we walked by, but it was hard. I didn't hear any sounds from their room this morning, thank god.

"So, where are we going?" I ask as soon as we're outside.

"For a walk."

I raise my eyebrows. "A walk?"

He nods with a shy smile.

"Lead the way."

We walk a couple of blocks before the sidewalk leads to a creek. The trail along the creek turns more rugged; soon, trees and water surround us instead of buildings.

The sun feels nice on my face as we walk. So does the silence, but Caius brought me here to say something, and I need to hear it.

"So...? What do you want to talk about?" I ask.

He takes a deep breath. "I'm sorry for being pushy with you before. It was wrong of me, and I shouldn't have. You clearly wanted Beckett, and I kept pushing. I just wanted to say I'm sorry."

"You're sorry because now that Beckett has proved what an ass he is, you still want a chance with me?"

He chuckles. "No, I just needed to tell you I'm sorry. I saw how much pain you were in last night, and I never want to be the cause of you being in that much distress. I like you a great deal, but I'm not the right man for you.

"But if I win the game, or if you chose me, I'll do everything in my power to help you—escape or be a good husband, if that's what you choose. Whatever happens, I just want to apologize. I fucked up, and I don't want to do it again."

"Your apology is accepted."

His shoulders slump in a relaxed manner. "Thank you."

"Is that all you wanted to talk about?"

He opens his mouth like he wants to say more. I know he does, but sharing his feelings is hard for him, and I'm not exactly making it easy.

"I want to help you, but I don't know how. Tell me

what you want. You want me to go kick Beckett's ass, kill him for hurting you? I will," he sputters out.

"You would kill the man your sister loves for me?"

He shrugs. "She could do better."

I smile at that. "Probably, but I still don't think you would do it. You love your sister too much, and I'm not blaming you for that."

"Then how do I help you with your father? Do I help you run? Do I help you win? What do you want?"

I sigh. "I can't run."

"Then how do I help you win?"

"Not sure, exactly. I doubt Vincent will let me win. Just ensure you and Ryker are the best choices for Vincent to pick. Show how strong you are. How good of a leader you are. How you won't take any crap from me and will be able to protect me, not how much you love or care for me.

"Show him how you can take over his place, how you're cruel and heartless. Ryker has that public image down. You could work on that some more. Stop coming off so charming and be more menacing."

His eyes are dark and sorrowful. "I'll do anything I can for you, Ri—anything."

We lock eyes, and there is so much unsaid between us —so much that will never be said.

I nod.

We finish our hike, talking about less serious things. We talk about which of the guys snores and which will find a girlfriend next. We talk about how nice the weather is. We talk about our favorite movies and books. We talk about anything that can distract us from our pain. His pain at losing his father and regaining his sister. My pain at losing the love of my life.

As we start heading back, I turn the conversation

serious once again. "I've thought of something else you can do."

"Anything," Caius repeats.

This is going to test his promise to me. "Try to find a way to stop the war between Beckett and his brother."

His smile drops, and he looks down at the dirt path we're walking on.

"I don't know why Beckett declared war, but he loves his brother, his family. He would do anything for them. Don't let him go to war," I plead.

Caius looks at me, dumbfounded. He wants to help me, but he can't promise me this.

"If not for Beckett's sake, then for your sister's. If Beckett goes to war, he'll never be the same. He'll be lost forever. If she wants a man who will love and protect her all her life, then he can't go to war. You have to help him put a stop to it."

Caius chews on his bottom lip for a second as my words sink in. "I'll see what I can do."

It's the best I'm going to get from him, so I don't push him further. We leave the creek trail and are back in town. It's a little early, but I don't want to return to the guys. I'm tired of saying goodbye.

"Take me to Vincent."

It feels strange stepping foot back in Vincent's swanky downtown penthouse. My head pounds—either from the pain of being back here or the fuzziness of my memories after Kek took me. I still don't remember much from the time Beckett almost killed me to when Kek took me. The guys filled me in some, but I feel like they all left out huge chunks of time, and I have no idea why.

What are they hiding from me?

I pour myself a glass of the nicest bottle of wine I can find and then make myself comfortable on the couch until Vincent makes his presence known.

I wait twenty minutes, but I don't mind. The silence is nice. I haven't had much of it since Caius rescued me. The guys are too afraid to leave me alone for a single second. I look down at the bracelet. It will stop working soon now that I'm safe. Ryker will have no need to protect me. I don't think the others will stop, though.

"So let's hear the brilliant game you've come up with," Vincent says, sitting on the edge of a nearby couch with his own glass of wine.

"I want the man I'm forced to marry to be the right man for me, not just the best man with a gun. So my game is a simple one—impress me with your words. Tell me why you deserve to marry me. What qualities do you possess that should make me pick you? Impress me. Tell me you love me if it's true or that you could love me. Declare your feelings for me."

Vincent just sips his wine. He hates my game and is going to come up with one of his own. This was a mistake. I should have come up with something more dangerous, then he might have gone along with it, and I would have some control.

"Or we could—"

Vincent cuts me off. "I like it. Simple, but an important task. We need a man who can speak, as well as he can shoot or lead. A leader's job is much more about speaking than shooting anyway."

"Really? You don't hate the idea?"

"Not at all." Vincent drinks more of his wine.

"And you'll let me choose the winner?"

"Of course, I think your opinion matters a great deal." There's a pause just long enough for me to feel like I've won. "But my opinion matters too."

My heart drops. "Of course," I mutter. I down the rest of my wine before standing and walking to the kitchen to pour myself another glass.

When I return, Vincent feels ready to drop a bigger bomb on me.

"Sit," he commands.

I take my seat again, afraid of what he's going to say.

"War is coming."

"Between the Retribution Kings and—"

"No, not just them. War in general. I've seen it come enough times now that I know when it's coming, and it's coming. You don't think I know why all these leaders entered this ridiculous game?"

"To win me?"

He chuckles. "To have a shot to take me down. They could either win and get my kingdom or try to use the game as a way to get close to me. Infiltrate my organization and kill me from within, but they've all failed so far."

"There have been attacks on you?" my mouth drops open at that thought.

"Of course. I made sure they all paid the price in the game. There is no need for these wars."

He sighs. "But war is coming. I've grown too powerful, and these young ones, especially, want more and more power. They aren't satisfied just to rule over their gangs and crews; they need more."

Vincent stands and walks over to a window, looking out. I can see the wrinkles on his face, the hairs that have all but turned grey, and the age that he used to carry so well weighing down on him. He's tired of leading, tired of being the ruler with great, terrifying power.

"What are you going to do?" I ask.

"We are strong. We can't be defeated by one or two rogue gang leaders. The only way we can be taken down is if they all work together. Only then will our armies fall."

"Do they realize that? Are they—"

"Yes, they are all cocky sons of bitches that think they are strong enough to take me down. They are starting to band together. I've seen the evidence of them meeting, of them trying to kill you in order to end my line. So far, their attempts have been futile. The ones leading the attacks aren't the smartest, but all it takes is one smart leader to join them, and then we'll fall."

I frown with my heart thumping wildly in my chest because I know how my father handles threats. I know how he handles attacks. And I don't like where this is headed.

"We need to take down as many leaders as possible. The strongest are left in this game, and we need to take as many down as possible before an uprising happens. We are so close to the end; I can't let anything interfere with my plans, not after everything we've sacrificed."

"I don't understand."

"Tonight, we kill half of them. We kill any that are a threat to us. We kill any that aren't on our side, any that could lead the others in war."

I gasp—*half.*

Half could include Caius.

It could include Ryker.

It could include Beckett. *No, Beckett won't come. He'll bow out.*

I suck in a breath. I need to change his mind. This is too much, too high of a chance of death.

"But the best leader among them is exactly who we want to lead the Corsi mafia. Wouldn't we be killing the best among them?"

"No, we don't want the best. We want the most loyal."

I stand and pace now. I can't let them die. I have to find a way to stop the death. None of the men left deserve to die.

"Won't their number twos come after us if we just kill men willy-nilly? It's one thing for them to die in competition, but it's another for us to just shoot them point-blank."

"We aren't going to shoot them; you are."

I frown. "I won't agree to shoot innocent people for no reason."

He laughs. "None of these men are innocent."

True. I'm running out of arguments.

"Why me?"

"I'm ready to unleash you, for the rest to see who you really are."

"And if I refuse?"

Don't say you'll kill Lucy, don't say you'll kill Beckett, don't say you'll kill...

"I'm not going to threaten you anymore."

"Then, what are you going to do?"

Vincent snaps his fingers, and Kek appears. I guessed he was working with my father to scare me or control me, but then I glance down to who he's holding in his arms—a limp Lucy, beaten and bruised.

"Lucy!" I run over to them.

"What happened?" I brush her hair out of her face and try not to wince when I see a large gash over her eye.

Lucy's bottom lip trembles, and she shivers in Kek's arms.

"Did you...?" I snap at Kek, assuming he's the monster behind this.

"It wasn't him," Vincent.

Lucy leans into his body like he alone will protect her, and I believe that Kek didn't hurt her.

"Then who?" I demand.

"That's what we are going to figure out. Only a limited number of people knew about the safe house—Ryker, Caius, and Beckett are at the top of the list."

My teeth grind together, but I know Vincent is right. One of them betrayed us. One of them did this to Lucy.

"I'm—" Lucy starts and then passes out in Kek's arms.

"Lucy!" I scream louder as I check her pulse. "I don't think she's breathing."

Kek lowers her onto the floor and starts performing CPR. Vincent calls for a medic, and I stand frantically by watching my only friend in the world—the only one I can truly trust—have her heart stop beating. I have no idea if she'll survive.

My blood rages through my body. Without a doubt in my mind, I'll kill anyone involved. It may play into my father's plan, but for once, we are on the same side.

22

BECKETT

THERE HAVEN'T BEEN many times in my life when I felt like I made the right choice. A sense of calm washes through me as I step into the restaurant; today I decided correctly.

Caius is on my left as we walk into the Italian restaurant owned by the Corsi family.

It took a lot of convincing the Retribution Kings to let me come, to keep competing since Odette is alive and I no longer have a need to win Rialta as my wife. But I told the Kings we still needed to finish the game, and I'd do everything in my power to help Caius win. I promised them if I somehow won, I'd have Caius or another member of the Retribution Kings marry Rialta. Corsi and controlling his kingdom are too important for me to bow out.

Ultimately, Odette was actually the one who convinced everyone I should go. I don't know what her motivations are. Maybe she wanted me to help protect her brother. Maybe she wants to see me dead. Or maybe there's something else going on I don't know about, but once she said I should go, there was no more discussion about it.

So here I am.

I have no idea why this game is taking place in one of their Italian restaurants, but at least we aren't decked out in tactical gear or arriving in the middle of the forest.

That has to be a good sign, right?

One of Corsi's men leads us through the empty restaurant to a back room where a large table has been set up. A few men are already sitting at the table as Caius and I take our seats. Ryker shows up next, but he pretends he doesn't know who we are. He sits next to one of the most ruthless men still in the game.

The table quickly fills up. Wine is poured. Bread is brought out. But still no sign of Ri or her father.

"Something's not right," I whisper to Caius after the main course is brought out.

"I agree. Do you think the game has already started, and they didn't tell us the rules?" Caius stares down at his food. "Like they poisoned the wine or food and want to see who has the strength to survive?"

"That seems farfetched. I more meant they were planning on starting the games at seven, like the text said, but had to move it back because something happened."

"You think something happened to Ri?" Caius asks, his face turning white instantly.

"I don't know, but something just doesn't feel right."

"Ryker put a tracker on her; maybe it's still active."

I glance across the table to where Ryker is. He laughs at something the man next to him says, acting like he doesn't have a care in the world.

But then Ryker's eyes meet mine.

I don't know how to communicate with him to tell him we're worried about Ri.

He looks down at his lap, and I realize he's on his

phone. I wait a minute to pull my phone out after I feel it buzz in my pocket. I don't want anyone to notice we are communicating. Before I can pull my phone out, the back doors open, and Corsi, Ri, and a third man enter the dining room.

"Holy fuck, that's Kek" Caius whispers next to me.

What the hell is going on?

All three of them take a seat at a table on the other side of the room facing us. I study Ri carefully, looking for any signs that her mind has been messed with, that she's been hurt, or is scared to death and sending signals for someone to help her. Instead, all I see is a ruthlessness in her eyes as she scans the room.

She starts her perusal on the other side of the table, looking at each man one by one. I don't know what she's so pissed about. I don't know what she's looking for in each of our eyes, but a small silence falls over the table under her gaze. Each man is being judged for his sins in her eyes.

She looks at Caius, and even he sinks down into his chair. She holds nothing back.

And then she looks at me. For a split second, her eyes widen and soften. There isn't the same hatred and pain she gave the other guys.

She's surprised I'm here.

A second later, that look is gone, replaced with the same heartless stare she gave everyone else. I've never seen Ri so furious.

She continues on until she has stared down every single one of us.

Corsi clears his throat, and the room goes silent. He doesn't move from his chair as he says, "Tonight's game is simple. You will meet with us, one at a time. Your task is to convince us that you should win, that you are worthy of my daughter. Only the top half will be advancing."

They are eliminating half of us. *The question is will the losing half get to live?*

Caius swallows hard next to me, and I suspect he's pondering the same question.

A name is called to their table, and then another course of food and wine is brought out. Conversation returns as the man takes a seat at the table and begins his interrogation—because I'm sure that's what it feels like.

Five minutes later, the guy returns to the table, looking completely unfazed. This is how it continues down the line. No one can really hear what the others are saying. The tables are too far away, and the sound of us chatting while we eat and drink drowns everything else out.

It's Caius's turn to be followed by mine.

I consider what I'm going to say.

What can I say?

I love you, Ri. I'm only staying with Odette to try and protect you from the guy you're currently sitting next to. The only reason I'm staying married to Odette is because she and Caius know the phrase that can be used to undo whatever Kek does to you.

Caius walks back to the table. He gives me no clue what he said or what happened. Now it's my turn.

I still don't know what I'm going to say as I approach the table. I came here to see if she's okay. Clearly, she's not okay. Something terrible happened, and I have no idea who to save her from.

"Have a seat, Beckett," Corsi says as I approach.

I take the seat across from them. Corsi doesn't show any emotion. Kek looks like he wants to murder me. And Ri—she looks completely lost when she looks at me.

It's then that I realize what I have to do. I have to stop leading her on. I have to put the final nail in her heart, severing her from me completely.

"You have five minutes to convince us why you should win and marry my daughter," Corsi says.

I take a deep breath, staring right at Ri. I came here to end this, to provide closure for both of us. I hope she can be with someone worthy of her, someone who deserves her.

"I shouldn't marry your daughter. I'm the last man who should."

Corsi's eyes raise, and Kek's face darkens, but Ri doesn't react to my words. She's strong and already knows what I'm about to say. I'm not even sure she needs to hear my words, but I need to say it out loud.

"I've betrayed her, hurt her, lied to her. I gave my heart to another woman who I thought had died. No, not died—I thought Ri killed her."

I look Ri dead in the eyes. "But I know that isn't true. My wife is alive. I'm a married man, which is one of the many reasons I'm not the right man for her. I'm not worthy of her. I'm not a good man. I suck as a leader. I let my emotions drive my actions. I failed to protect her time and time again.

"But the number one reason I'm not the one for your daughter—I'm in love with another woman."

I wait for Corsi to chew me out. I wait for Ri to ask me to resign from the games. Neither happens.

"Thank you, your time is up," Corsi says.

I stand and turn to head back to my spot, unsure what's going to happen until I hear Kek speak.

"He's a dead man."

RI

I TRIED to listen to the men when they all stated they were the ones for me. Several insisted they were the best choice because they were the most vicious, cruel man around— not exactly what I wanted to hear. Some said they were madly in love.

Ryker was harsh and controlling with his words. He pretended to think of me as nothing more than a possession, something to control. He said we both have a role to play, and he knew his. Everything he said was the complete opposite of the man I knew.

Caius ignored my advice. Instead of acting like Ryker, Caius was sweet, charming, a love-sick boy who professed his love for me.

And Beckett was...honest, devastatingly honest.

Why did he come?

He should have just quit; now there's a strong chance he'll die for what he just said.

There has to be a reason Beckett came; I just can't figure out what it is. I can't figure out anything when it comes to him.

"So, who wins and who loses?" Kek asks us.

I stare at Vincent, unsure of what happens next. There was no obvious culprit who hurt Lucy, but someone here did.

"What do you think, Ri?" Vincent asks.

"I honestly don't know who hurt Lucy, and that's all I care about at the moment. Not professions of love. Not who is the strongest, badass guy around. I just want to punish whoever hurt Lucy; the rest can live."

Vincent nods. "It's not about killing the right person. It's about setting an example that we won't tolerate this. We will kill until we get answers."

I frown as a tear slips. "It matters to me."

"We'll make sure the right person pays, but for now, we just need to show our power."

I look at him, knowing what happens next. "Who do you want me to kill?"

"Three, any three."

I stare him down, shocked he's giving me this power.

"They're all armed. What do I do when they retaliate?"

"They won't. We'll make it clear we have evidence of them scheming together to kill Lucy. It will stop them from working together in the future against us."

I'm not sure it will, but I need to know who hurt Lucy.

"You'll let me do this my way? I'll kill whoever I think is responsible for Lucy's death?"

"You have my word. Show them how strong you are. Show them what won't be tolerated."

"What's changed? Why do I no longer have to play the princess part?"

"We are close to the end, and I need the men to see who you truly are."

I look to Kek, a man I fear. A man who can wipe my memories in a single second—I may need him to after what I'm about to do.

"How do I get them to confess?" I ask.

Kek has tortured me, and I'm sure countless others. He knows how to pull confessions out of people.

He smirks. "You already know how."

I frown, not really sure what he's saying.

"If everyone could line up against the wall, we'd like to announce the winners," Vincent announces.

The men stand casually and walk to a wall to be picked as the winner. Only a couple seem weary. Ryker, Caius, and Beckett all know what's about to happen, but they do as they're asked. I doubt they will fight their fates. All of them are prepared to die.

Kek, Vincent, and I take our time standing and walking over in front of them.

"Rialta will do the announcing of winners. Rialta," Vincent says, giving me the floor.

Two of the guys give me a flirtatious wink; I ignore them.

"Listen up," I snap with my full voice, and I know I've got their full attention. "My best friend, Lucy, was seriously injured. Right now, she's unconscious, fighting for her life." My voice pours with pain and desperation.

I walk up and down the line, staring at each of them. "I'm giving you one chance. If you know anything about who hurt Lucy, tell me now."

I continue to walk up and down the line of men. I stare at Ryker, Caius, Beckett. One of them has to know something. One of them might have even been the one to hurt her.

A man, I think his name is Nigel, steps forward from the line. I don't know much about him, except he's a cruel man. From the speech he gave me, he doesn't think highly of women.

I don't hesitate.

I pull my gun and fire into his chest.

I watch the shock appear on his face, the whites in his eyes grow wider, and then he falls hard to the ground.

No one moves.

I expect them all to reach for their guns. I expect an all-out war to start. Vincent was right, though—show my power, and they all fear me.

"Anyone else have anything to say about what happened to Lucy?" I ask.

No one moves a muscle.

I'm not sure what I should do next.

I turn, and Vincent looks at me sternly, egging me on. If I don't choose more to kill, he will, and that scares the shit out of me.

I grab Kek's arm, and we take a step back, far enough away from the line that they can't hear me.

"I don't know what to do," I say.

Kek looks at me. "And you're asking me? The guy you fear more than anything?"

"I don't fear you, not anymore."

I look over my shoulder and see Beckett out of the corner of my eye. He's the only man I care to save, even if it kills me.

"Is he a good man?" Kek asks me, talking about Beckett.

"The best." Even if he doesn't always seem like it, I know who he is deep down.

"Then he can never be yours."

I turn, staring back at Kek. "What do you mean?"

He sighs. "You have to give him up."

"What if I can't?" I whisper, tears coming, assuming he means give him up to Odette.

"Kill him now if you can't give him up. He'll never be yours."

It's the most honest thing anyone has ever said to me.

He puts his fingers under my chin and looks deep into my eyes. "For what it's worth, I think you're strong enough to give him up, strong enough to let him live with another."

I blink back my tears, refusing to cry.

"I need you to erase my memories. Erase him completely from my head. That's the only way I'll survive watching him with another woman."

Kek looks at me sadly. "I already tried and failed. Even when I erased the best of him, you still loved him."

I frown. "What do you mean?"

"You need to kill two more men."

"I don't know how to choose."

"You do. You know exactly who your greatest threats are. You know who hurt Lucy. You know. Deep down, you know."

I run my hand through my hair. I do, but...*can I do it?*

We walk back toward the line of men, and I look at each of them again.

Ryker looks bored.

Caius looks concerned.

Beckett looks at peace, ready to die.

Two more men have to die.

I know exactly which two.

Then Kek whispers in my ear the phrase I hate. But this time I'm thankful because he gives me everything back. "Kill all those who are a threat to you and trust your gut."

I know which two have to die.

Both deaths are hard.

But one I know to be a sinner. He's hurt me time and time again.

The other, I'm just realizing how much of a saint he is.

Both are threats to me.

Both have to die.

I thought one didn't love me.

I was wrong.

And now two people are going to die for my mistake.

I lift my gun and fire twice.

Two lives have ended.

And I'll never be the same again.

———

Thank you so much for reading Fatal Princess! Ri and Beckett's story continues in Tortured Hero.

JOIN ELLA'S NEWSLETTER & NEVER MISS A
SALE OR NEW RELEASE → ellamiles.com/freebooks

Love swag boxes & signed books?
SHOP MY STORE → store.ellamiles.com

ALSO BY ELLA MILES

LIES SERIES:

Lies We Share: A Prologue

Vicious Lies

Desperate Lies

Fated Lies

Cruel Lies

Dangerous Lies

Endless Lies

SINFUL TRUTHS:

Sinful Truth #1

Twisted Vow #2

Reckless Fall #3

Tangled Promise #4

Fallen Love #5

Broken Anchor #6

TRUTH OR LIES:

Taken by Lies #1

Betrayed by Truths #2

Trapped by Lies #3

Stolen by Truths #4

Possessed by Lies #5

Consumed by Truths #6

DIRTY SERIES:

Dirty Obsession

Dirty Addiction

Dirty Revenge

Dirty: The Complete Series

ALIGNED SERIES:

Aligned: Volume 1 (Free Series Starter)

Aligned: Volume 2

Aligned: Volume 3

Aligned: Volume 4

Aligned: The Complete Series Boxset

UNFORGIVABLE SERIES:

Heart of a Thief

Heart of a Liar

Heart of a Prick

Unforgivable: The Complete Series Boxset

MAYBE, DEFINITELY SERIES:

Maybe Yes

Maybe Never

Maybe Always

Definitely Yes

Definitely No

Definitely Forever

STANDALONES:

Pretend I'm Yours

Pretend We're Over

Finding Perfect

Savage Love

Too Much

Not Sorry

Hate Me or Love Me: An Enemies to Lovers Romance Collection

ABOUT THE AUTHOR

Ella Miles writes steamy romance, including everything from dark suspense romance that will leave you on the edge of your seat to contemporary romance that will leave you laughing out loud or crying. Most importantly, she wants you to feel everything her characters feel as you read.

Ella is currently living her own happily ever after near the Rocky Mountains with her high school sweetheart husband. Her heart is also taken by her goofy five year old black lab who is scared of everything, including her own shadow.

Ella is a USA Today Bestselling Author & Top 50 Best-selling Author.

Stalk Ella at:
www.ellamiles.com
ella@ellamiles.com